DEEP SECRETS

WILLIAM SALMOND

WRITERS REPUBLIC L.L.C.
515 Summit Ave. Unit R1
Union City, NJ 07087, USA

Website: *www.writersrepublic.com*
Hotline: *1-877-656-6838*
Email: *info@writersrepublic.com*

Ordering Information:
Quantity sales. Special discounts are available on quantity purchases by corporations, associations, and others. For details, contact the publisher at the address above.

Library of Congress Control Number: 2020943023
ISBN-13:   978-1-64620-400-7   [Paperback Edition]
                  978-1-64620-401-4   [Digital Edition]

Rev. date: 08/04/2020

In fondest memory of Anne, who shared each intriguing step of our African odyssey. Your legacy, Anne, lives on in new, surprising ways.

Acknowledgements

Each of you, dear reader, was produced in about nine months. This book took a little longer - more like five years.

I am grateful to my friend and mentor Tag Mendillo, screenwriter and movie producer, for support, advice and encouragement during many cups of coffee in Las Vetas café.

Thanks to Writers Republic for their patience and professionalism.

Grey Lynden, Fulfilment officer, Arthur Mendoza, Publishing Consultant, Matt Alasagas, Cover Design, and Khervin Coleta, Interior Design.

Many thanks.

When I suffer in my mind, stories are my
refuge; I take them like opium, and
consider one who writes them a sort of doctor of the mind.
—Robert Louis Stevenson.

Sometimes a kind of glory lights up the mind of
man. I guess a man's importance in the world can be
measured by the quality and number of his glories.
—John Steinbeck

The kingdom of heaven is like a merchant in search of
fine pearls, who, when he had found one pearl of great
price went and sold all that he had and bought it.
—Jesus in Matthew 13:45–46
(Revised Standard Version)

Part 1

Chapter

1

Glorious yet far from glory. Winslow sat on his spacious verandah dressed simply in bright-yellow running shirt, tan shorts, and sneakers. A pair of Dr. Scholls inserts helped protect his ankle bones from the wear and tear of running. The verandah seats were between two huge tubs glowing with Landscape Solutions' carefully cared-for pink and scarlet begonias. He stared out at the sparkling waters of Long Island Sound and wondered for the umpteenth time about his luck at owning such a residence. "Gold Coast," the realtors called the area. And this particular home with glorious views was perched cliff high, storm safe, on a promontory jutting proudly oceanward. Obsessive hard work and some luck with his publications, especially *Money Matters*, had made it all possible. He developed an almost hypnotic stare as he reflected on all he had—respect, power, and certainly wealth beyond the wildest dreams of ordinary people. He was proud that his mother, now into her nineties was comfortably taken care of with him. He had lost count of the number of people from a wide range of companies that kept this one house, plus his mother, functioning. But still something was missing. Something as close to life as life itself. A touch, a word, a glimpse of glory.

"Penny for your thoughts, Win?"

Winslow smiled as his mother Eleanor joined him. Only she called him Win.

"You look terrific, Mother." Winslow admired his mother's impeccable dress sense. Even on this hot fall day she looked cool in sweat pants and dramatic-colored top. No one ever believed that she had recently celebrated her ninetieth birthday. Her gray eyes sparkled in unison with the sun on the waves.

"Yes, I seem always to be preoccupied these days."

"About what?"

"Well, apart from this damn virus which has unraveled our economy, I've been thinking a lot lately about your great-granddaughter."

"Eleanor. You know, never a day goes by that I don't spend some time wondering about her." Winslow began to wax whimsical as if in a dream. "Lately, since coming out of my cardiac procedure, I've had so many flashbacks. Somehow my subconscious mind has been swept open. She and I in the garden. She loved catching leaves before they landed on the lawn. She was always concerned if I had a little cut on my hand, and she would kiss it better. I wonder if she still has the pink teddy I gave her. You know the one with one left ear."

Eleanor laughed. "She had a tug of war with Rex over it, and Rex got the ear."

"Mmm, the right one."

"Yes, the right one. Funny detail but true."

"Then the game of her on a scooter that crashes. She falls. 'Catch me, Grandpa!' she yells. I miss her. She falls unconscious, and I call an ambulance. She is put in a hospital bed, mouth open, tongue out. After a shot and a tablet, she is just fine again. 'Again, Grandpa, again,' she yells. One weekend she left pink teddy at our house. When she returned, she asked me, 'Did you sleep with teddy, Grandpa?' I told her, 'No, I sleep with Grandma!'"

Winslow froze at the utterance of this final word.

Eleanor with her lovely gift of silence just gazed seaward.

"Been over a year now," Winslow muttered to a scurrying squirrel. "God help us. Martha Jane's illness was too long. I still think her bipolar lithium meds had something to do with her cancer. We gave it everything." His raised voice reverberated over the fall leaves. "Everything."

"Cancer, Win. It often gets us in the end." She leaned over and held his hand. "Listen! You were superb all the way through, especially in the final weeks when Martha Jane was in hospice. Thank you for that."

Mother and son gazed seaward and stopped talking for some moments.

Then Eleanor said, "So many memories are flooding back now."

"You spend too much time on them, Mother. Think ahead," Winston advised.

"What have I to look forward to? Memories are my archive, you know! I'd give anything to see her again before, well, before the end. She would be going on eighteen by now. Thank God at least I have this beautiful home to enjoy my sunset years in."

Winslow closed his eyes. "You know, even if we found Eleanor, I doubt she would forgive me."

"Tough thing, forgiveness. Not sure I've yet forgiven your pop, you know."

Winslow stood up and stretched his arms skyward. "Don't talk about your end. The only person near death in this house is me, which reminds me, I have my post-cardiac rehab soon."

Before his mother could reply, Winslow grabbed his iPhone. "Jeannie, I mean, Madame Secretary."

"Not a social call, Winslow. Tonight. Washington. Just you and me."

"Me?" he asked.

"Yes, and before you ask, our Somalia sortie failed."

"Who was that?" her mother asked.

Winslow shrugged. "No details. She sounds worried. Jeannie Backhouse wants to talk to me tonight in Washington."

"You two should have married, you know. Perfect for each other. Don't know what happened."

"Life happened, Mother. Life. It tends to get in the way of all our plans...and our ambitions. Me, I'm just another cog in the money wheels of the Federal Reserve. Now they are talking of retiring a few of us off. For me the chair job and the haloed Basle trips are just a pipe dream. Thank God for *Money Matters*."

"You know, I don't think you have a mystical bone in that body of yours. Numbers, numbers, numbers. Who cares about stupid numbers? So Apple is valued at nearly a trillion dollars in New York. So? So? But it employs only a quarter as many people as the world's largest company PetroChina. So fewer people making more money. Is that good?"

Acerbic mind. Acerbic tongue. Winslow smiled.

But like a grain of sand that slips between the two shells of an oyster, her words itched and turned. An incipient mystical pearl? His mother was now in full flow.

"What happened to your heritage? Your grandfather had the second sight, you know?"

"Nope."

"He called me the night your father walked into Long Island Sound. 'Something's wrong,' he told me. 'Something bad. Look for Winston.' Two days later you found his body on the shore. Too late, but my father knew. He knew."

Mother and son contemplated this first family catastrophe. Neither dared voice the more disastrous second. Eleanor changed the subject.

"When you get a minute, and I don't suppose you ever get many minutes these days, take a look at this screenplay. Someone sent it to me. Says she needs an angel investor to take it to the screen."

"Mother you are an angel, a real soft touch. But please don't be taken in by all these requests. Your publishing house is sold. Throw it away."

Eleanor shook her head. "No, Win, I won't. You see it's a love story."

Winslow grimaced. "Love? For me? I don't think a stupid screenplay will do it."

Eleanor was nothing if not persistent. "Win, you need to develop a more whimsical, mystical nature. Do you realize there is a very strong relationship between human spirituality and human sexuality?"

"Nope." Winslow rolled his eyes.

"Listen to the master poet William Butler Yeats. 'My soul had found all happiness in its own cause or ground. Godhead on Godhead in sexual spasm begot Godhead.' You see, mysticism and sensuality are closely intertwined."

Win groaned. He was now becoming worried about the flights of fancy of his mother. Mother the publisher, mother the writer and reader, mother the lover of the poems of William Butler Yeats was light-years from his numbers-grounded life.

"What's the screenplay called?" he asked.

"*Journey to the Heart.* Based on a true story. Florence is a Hungarian slave girl in nineteenth- century Ottoman Empire. She is rescued in Viddin on the Danube during a slave auction by Samuel Baker, an English widower, and together they travel from Egypt down the Nile to discover one of the Nile's sources in Africa, Lake Albert in Uganda. En route they become lovers, then return to England and marry. It's lovely, Win, real lovely. Look at this piece…"

Winslow reluctantly took the manuscript and read it. He found himself humoring his mother more as she aged.

*****

EXT. THE RIVER NILE (WHITE NILE) SNAKING ITS WAY OUT OF KHARTOUM. ON BOARD A SAILING BARGE—MORNING

Sam has engaged three vessels for the journey south. Two sailing barges, or *noggurs*, and a decked *diahbiah*, or paddle steamer with a comfortable cabin. The boats are loaded with provisions for four months, plus extra corn and supplies in case they meet up with fellow explorers, Speke and Grant. They have twenty-one donkeys and four camels on the boats. Sam has hired forty soldiers, whom he has taught to march to the drum, and Florence is busy onboard sewing uniforms for them. She calls them the Forty Thieves of Ali Baba! Plus forty men to work as sailors and ten servants. Sam has also hired a German carpenter, Johann Schmidt, to be headman, or *vakeel*, making a total of ninety-eight expedition members. All the men are Arabs except the black African, Richarn.

> FLORENZ
> Almost finished the uniforms for the forty thieves, Sam!
> SAMUEL BAKER
> Let's hope they don't turn out that way, Flori.

Sam is busy opening mail, which has just been delivered to Khartoum.

> SAMUEL BAKER (CONT'D)
> Oh, good heavens!
> FLORENZ
> What's wrong?
> SAMUEL BAKER
> Look at this *London Times* story. The Prince Consort, Albert,
> Queen Victoria's beloved Albert, died four months ago.
> FLORENZ
> I am sorry for her. She owns the world,
> but now she has lost her heart.
> SAMUEL BAKER
> A very long mourning period has been declared. The queen
> has retired to Balmoral Castle in Scotland—inconsolable.
> FLORENZ
> What does that big word mean in your funny English?
> SAMUEL BAKER
> It means no one is able to comfort her.

Screams and shouts as a school of hippos rise and edge the last barge into the air. A donkey falls off and is immediately attacked by a crocodile and dragged under the river. Blood rises to the surface.

*****

"Mr. Kirk."

Winston handed the manuscript back to his mother and looked up.

"I came round the side way and saw you were on the verandah."

"So much for our top security apparatus, which only works inside the house."

Winslow looked from her bright-blue sneakers up to her very short tan shorts and a tight- fitting light-blue top. Her blond hair was held back in a ponytail.

"I'm Doris, sir, from Coast Agency."

Winslow shook her hand. "Mother, this is a nurse for my post-cardiac rehab."

"I suppose lesser mortals have to do all this in hospital but not our Win. He has his own gym and now his very own nurse. Your dad would be pleased. 'Win, win, win,' he always said and a lot of good that did him."

The young woman blushed. She was not used to be party to such personal family secrets.

"Shall we, sir?"

"Please call me Winslow."

As they walked into the house, Doris stopped at the begonias.

"So lovely. You know they have special meaning?"

"Nope."

"They are a warning about future events. Sometimes misfortunes. Sometimes challenges we have to face."

Winslow stared at her. "Are you a nurse or a fortune-teller?"

"I worked in a garden nursery while doing my nursing studies. These colors are truly dramatic, you know."

"So what do they tell us?"

"Pink and scarlet. So special. They depict romance and love."

"What mumbo jumbo."

Winslow hurried into the house, but Doris stopped again in the hallway.

"Beautiful paintings," she murmured as she glanced at the two paintings hanging prominently side by side. "Early American Impressionist?"

Winslow's surprise spoke volumes on his rugged face.

"I studied art history at Bowdoin College in Maine, then ran out of money and returned to nursing to pay off the student loans. One day I'll go back, maybe."

Winslow grinned. "Well, you are right. Frank Benson is the artist. That's his daughter Eleanor, age nine. Someone once wrote of him that he dips his brush into a little jar marked 'sunshine.' The one on the right is the same daughter Eleanor, age seventeen. He calls it *Sunlight*."

Doris spent some time admiring the excellent paintings.

"Yes, I love the way he uses light to tell us something about the soul of his little girl. I wonder where they were painted?"

"He painted them on Wooster Farm on New Haven Island in Maine," Winslow explained. "Both originals by the way. Since my security system is so useless, you might as well have dropped in and picked them up. My mother nearly bankrupted me that year. She and I actually went there to see his home."

"Why?"

A simple question but deep and perceptive. Why indeed? Doris and Winslow stood looking back toward the open porch doors and the sea.

"Look, it's none of my business. Let's get to the gym. I'm sorry."

Suddenly Winslow was in no hurry.

"It's okay. You have touched on a very sensitive nerve in this family. Eleanor was the name of my granddaughter who was given up for adoption after her mother and father died. My mother and I find these some kind of comfort. Like Eleanor in the painting, my granddaughter would be almost eighteen by now."

Winslow stopped the musings by leading the way down into his basement gym. Doris set up her equipment and began placing plastic markers on his chest: green marker, right; red, over the heart to the left; and white, above near the right collar bone. Winslow held his shirt up and closed his eyes as her nimble young fingers put each one in place. How long had it been he wondered since he had felt a woman's sensual touch? Too long, he concluded. Each wire led to a black instrument attached on his belt, which would relay details of his pulse to Doris' laptop screen.

She then took his blood pressure and recorded it on her laptop.

"It's 140 over 80. Could be worse. We'll do this again while you are exercising and then when you finish. Remember all this is to help mend your heart."

Winslow said nothing but told himself that nothing and no one could mend this heart of his. Heartbreak was heartbreak, and all the king's horses and all the king's men could never put him together again.

Doris took this silence as a sign to explain further. She held her thumb and forefinger very close together.

"You were this close to a heart attack, sir, er, Winslow. Your left anterior descending coronary artery, which nourishes the largest part of your heart muscle, was 95 percent blocked by plaque. And a second was nearly as bad. Now the cardiac bypass, which the surgeon has put in place, will allow a new and steady blood flow. My job is to help get you back to your normal fitness and life."

Winslow nodded, stepped on his treadmill, and cranked it up to 3.6 mph fast walking.

"In the hospital this morning, we were discussing how soon after heart procedures patients can resume sexual activity. So here at home I will share the same discussion with you."

"Sex! What the hell has sex got to do with anything! Do we get a certificate saying we can start again?"

Doris took a step backward. She was used to touching not just men's chests but also raw nerves and bruised egos. In a steady conversational tone, she continued, "Usually a month or six weeks after the procedure our clients can resume sexual activity if they so desire. For older men like you, sex would be the equivalent of climbing three flights of stairs."

"Well, thanks very much! So for the younger ones, it would be more like a simple stroll in the park!"

"No, not really. Not really. It's much the same for all." She was now sorry she had added the proviso about his age. She wondered if she would ever marry. How could anyone handle such weak creatures with huge egos?

Winslow cranked the treadmill up to 4.6 mph and began running.

"So sex can cause a heart attack, is that what you are saying?"

"No, sir. Only six out of a thousand heart attack sufferers die of heart attack during sex but..."

"Come on, Doris, what's the catch? What's the big but?"

Doris showed all her ivory white teeth. "But 80 percent of these are cheating on their partners when they die."

"Way to go," Winslow muttered. "Anyway I don't have a partner to cheat on."

Moving over to the cross trainer and putting the resistance up to level 6, Winston said, "Begonias. Misfortunes or challenges?"

"Sometimes both, Winslow, or just one of the two."

"I'll take challenges any day. My grandfather told me that when he left the Royal High School the rector—you know, principal—told all the boys—was a boys-only school then—that life was a challenge. He was very proud of his school in Edinburgh, Scotland, and told me that it was the first to ever worldwide to record the name 'high school.' This was in the year 1505."

"Wow, even older than you, Winslow," Doris teased and punched his moving arm.

"You have many challenges in your work in the Federal Reserve. I mean the world post coronavirus is so scary nowadays. Everything so uncertain."

"The world I can handle, Doris. It's me that's the real problem."

"Win!" A shrill voice from above.

"Mother."

"When you've stopped schmoozing with that young thing down there, I need you to pay my three carers."

Winslow stepped off the cross trainer.

Doris guided his hand to remove the now sweaty disks attached to his chest. A few hairs held them longer than normal. What was normal? Winston held her hand.

"Thank you for your help. I appreciate it."

Doris held his gaze. "You're welcome. And remember you are still in recovery. No sex, yet. Not too much excitement and restricted travel makes sense." She then giggled. "The certificate we mentioned could be available in a few weeks."

Was this a promise? As Winston made his way upstairs, he wondered at the complexity of his private life. From time to time he had opportunities for sex and maybe a deeper relationship, but fear of any change held him back. Numbers didn't have emotional swings and roundabouts, and he found them more consistent, hence comforting. Then he smiled as he recalled Doris' 80 percent figure and looked forward to sharing it over drinks with friends.

As he passed the begonias, he winked at them. "Romance. Love. Bring it on, begonias. Bring it on."

Chapter

2

"Lordy, Lordy. Surprise me, Lord. What's the secretary of state wanting with a number cruncher in the Federal Reserve?"

Winslow Kirk muttered this prayer as he sat in a cab hurtling down Pennsylvania Avenue toward the White House.

The fact that he prayed at all was unusual. The last time might have been at his wife, Martha Jane's funeral over a year ago or after the boating fiasco that had changed his life forever. Also this was not really his prayer. It was the prayer of his grandfather from the pulpit of his kirk in the village of Duddingston in Edinburgh, Scotland. Winslow could still feel the cold of the stone walls, the hushed atmosphere, the mix of awe and some fear in the faces of those around him. Winslow was then ten and stayed with his grandparents for a year after his own father's sudden death while his mother finished a college degree in literature and publishing and tried to rebuild their lives over the pond in Connecticut. Winslow could still see the towering figure of his grandfather, his white beard in striking contrast to his jet-black robes. His voice, with no modern microphone assistance, bounced off the stone walls and kept everyone in church very much awake.

"Let us pray in unison, 'Surprise me, Lord.'"

Winslow could still hear the rolling *r*'s in his grandfather's voice.

"Lor-r-rd."

Arriving back at the manse, he had found a brand-new bicycle propped beside a large bed of salmon-pink-tinged yellow rosebushes named "Peace."

"You see, laddie, the Lord is full of surprises," his grandfather told him.

This was the other side of his austere grandfather. His bright sea-blue eyes twinkled with fun, even mischief.

The cab screeched to a halt outside The Old Ebbitt Bar and Grill opposite the White House. Winslow put a magazine back on the seat where he had found it. He had completed only the first question of its "Life Coach Questionnaire."

When all aspects of your life seem to be falling apart simultaneously, do you perceive this as:
a) Just dumb bad luck
b) A mystery which is part of life's rich and varied tapestry
c) Your own stupid fault
d) A unique opportunity for the growth of the trillion-dollar industries of alcohol, tobacco, sleep aids, anti-anxiety drugs

The number cruncher in the Federal Reserve System had ticked all four boxes.

Many think that the affairs of state of the American people and the world are conducted within the iconic Capitol building in the heart of the nation's capital, Washington. Samuel Adams, the maître d' of The Old Ebbitt Bar and Grill opposite the White House, knew differently.

"Good evening, Chairman." His gravelly voice was strong and welcoming. His deep-gray eyes were inquisitive and sensitive to all changes of mood, the slightest of nuances. For close on fifteen years, he had stood guard over the bar and cuisine of the only Washington establishment that came close to a British club. Like a British butler, he was both caring yet confident. He had watched the rise and fall of many administrations and had somehow retained the trust of each person who entered the restaurant. Nearly six feet tall, Sam was resplendent as ever in his gray coat and tails.

Chairman? Like Macbeth's witches' prophecy, "And shalt be king hereafter," was this a promise of future greatness? Winslow grunted an acknowledgment of the maître d's presence.

"The Secretary is on her way, sir. Great news on the al-Shabaab strike. A drone a day keep the terrorists at bay! Did we get Abu Ubaidah, the emir?"

Winslow said nothing. All customers at The Old Ebbitt Bar and Grill understood that Sam often knew more about the affairs of the nation than many of their colleagues in Congress and Senate. The secretary of state had recently recommended that the president authorize the establishment of an expansion of America's combined Air and Space Operations Center in the desert of Qatar, where three digital maps carry tracking details of every aircraft, civilian and military in the skies over Syria, Persian Gulf, and Afghanistan. This expansion would include Africa, but unlike its big brother in Qatar, the Africa location was still top secret—well, kind of secret. Sam had told customers it was in Djibouti, East Africa. Secret? A short time later the Chinese had then established their own military and research nearby. Then United Arab Emirates had developed a base for their troops. Had the maître d' tipped them off?

Winslow matched the maître d's height but was much more muscular. His dark curly hair, though thinning faster than he would have liked, was his pride and joy, always slightly unkempt in a deliberate kind of way and always trying to cover a couple of these pesky bald patches. His winter-sky blue eyes met those of Sam Adams.

"Classified. Tonight the corner table, as far from prying eyes and ears as possible in the alcove. Just for two, the Secretary and myself."

Winslow almost threw his deep-navy London Fog at the maître d' and gratefully eased his large frame into a leather chair in the deepest recess of the dark-paneled restaurant. Paintings of English hunting scenes decorated the wall above his head, mirroring the present-day hunt for the fox, Abu Ubaidah, the emir and leader of al-Shabaab in Somalia. His extraordinary finesse also served as a dynamic liaison among many al-Qaeda terror groups such as Boko Haram, who had recently caused such mayhem in West Africa and were moving south through Burkina Faso to Ghana. He now acted as a bridge as he seemed to share the DNA of each terror group, an evil rapprochement. Rumored also to be the next head of al-Qaeda, he was now the United States' number one terror target.

"Maker's Mark, not too many rocks."

Sipping his drink, Winslow enjoyed a few blissful moments of actually being alone. But his reflections brought him no reprieve. He gazed at the cornered fox and the baying hounds. The Secretary, in her call to him, had answered the maître d's question. With the president's final approval, they had moved in. The *Predator* (called Jambo) was launched, and with its rear-mounted propeller spinning efficiently, it cruised at 10,000 feet at a speed of 135 mph using its 48.7 foot wingspan for perfect balance. The strike hit the target, a shack beside a small rural mosque in the outskirts of Marka in southern Somalia. Perfect. Bin Laden, gone; al-Baghdadi, gone; Sulaimani, gone; and now Abu Ubaidah? But then the CIA's informants had vanished, and all contact with them lost, so there was now no way to confirm the success, or otherwise, of the strike.

"Damn it to hell," he told the bottom of his glass. "Better freshen this one up, Sam," he growled.

Sam moved toward the well-stocked bar.

"Hello, Buttsy." Secretary of State Jeannie Backhouse grinned as she followed behind Sam and the senator's refreshed drink.

Winslow stood and stooped down to hug the Secretary, about half a foot below him. Every time he saw her, he could only think of the front cover of a fashion mag. *Petite, was that the word?* he thought. Her blond hair was short, businesslike, but sexy in its own controlled snowstorm way.

Winslow tucked her under the chin.

"Chin up. You okay? Buttsy? Can't you be a bit more respectful?"

Jeannie smiled. "I can still see you headbutting the boys who teased you. A real goat!"

"My dad's death drove me crazy. Mom tried, but we were ever broke."

"Don't answer this if you don't want to, but what really happened with your father?"

Winslow stared at a fox in a distant painting. "He was cornered like a hunted fox. He was part of a gambling syndicate and got deep into debt. By the time he was pulled out of Long Island Sound, Mom and I were also underwater. To the tune of $40,000. Lost our house too. He used title deeds for his final dice throw. How the hell Mom pulled us back to sanity, I'll never know."

Jeannie shook her head. "You know what Dostoevsky said in *The Gambler*. 'Is it really possible to touch a gaming table without being infected at once with superstition?' I'm sorry."

The two friends were silent.

Then Winslow continued, "I don't think much of the teasing anymore. Hell, I've come a long way from it all. From taunts of poor boy to wealth, from bullying in middle school to a respected position in the Fed."

Jeannie ordered a large Domaine de Montille Burgundy and examined the large leather menu.

"Myself, okay? No, I'm not okay, Win. More like ko-knock-out punches. The divorce is concluded, but that was last week's crisis. Now it's my mother. I thought the coronavirus was behind us, but she has tested positive up in Portland, and I will need to visit in protective wear. She's not responding well, and oxygen level is dropping. I just delayed my East Africa trip again after these bombings," she said. "Seems my life is unraveling in perfect symmetry with our crazy world."

Winslow nodded. He knew Jeannie's husband and thought of her as the sandwich wife. The second wife of hedge fund guru, Casey Mace, Jeannie had become caught between the history of wife one and the media circus of wife three.

"By the way, Casey's third is already featuring in *People* and other mags. A Sharapova look-alike from Bulgaria. At least now I'm free to turn my attention to the unraveling world," she said. Then straight to business. "Winslow, things have happened at the Fed."

Winslow interrupted her. "No need to tell me. Sam told me I was promoted to Chairman."

Jeannie looked embarrassed. "Sorry. I simply told him when I reserved that I was meeting with the Chairman."

"Not possible. What about, Chuck?'

"Massive heart attack this morning. He died almost immediately."

"Shit. Sorry to hear that. I walked the beach with him last week. He seemed just fine after his recent bypass surgery."

"Worse than that, he wasn't at home. Found in a Trump Tower Hotel suite with a call girl."

Winslow nodded. He thought of what Doris had told him that morning. Those cheating on their wives were 80 percent more likely to succumb to a second heart attack.

"But his deputy is Elwood Caswell."

Jeannie squirmed in her seat and raised her right hand to Sam, indicating that an urgent refill was necessary.

Why is life so complicated, she wondered, *for all of us?*

"Look, Winslow, I have to be so careful. This is down to the secretary of the Treasury, and he is the one to tell you more. Come by the office early tomorrow, and we'll finish that part of the crisis. But tonight is a completely different matter. Sure, I invited you to dinner. But this is Washington, the city of intrigue. And I, of course, have an ulterior motive. I need your help. In the last few days, I have been brought into a very small group comprising some top intelligence chiefs, two top military boys, and President Kamala herself. I will not give you details. Such information is always known around here as 'deep secrets.' Anyway, it's bad and terror planning is truly underway once again. It seems that as we were tackling the coronavirus crisis, many of the most hardened

Islamic State fighters have made a breakout from Ghourian jail and a few other sites guarded by the Kurdish forces in northeast Syria. The Kurds were doing an excellent job there controlling up to ten thousand Islamic State prisoners. But of course, with Turkey's invasion of Syria, the Kurds have been weakened and, well, total chaos. The escapees have been moving south to Yemen, then into Somalia to join with al-Shabaab. Our drone strike killed a few villagers but not Abu. Some children were also killed. We have stirred up a hornets' nest, and we understand that the terror planning has accelerated. Anyway, this is where you come in. There have been some strange money transfers in the region through Pearl of Africa Bank in Kampala, Uganda. A small bank but recent money flow through it has been out of all proportion to its size. I think it may be terror related. Of course, it could also be just good old-fashioned greed and money laundering for oligarchs. I was wondering if you could call the governor of the Bank of Uganda and ask him to shut it down."

Winslow blinked. The childhood sweethearts stared at the wall hangings.

Then Winslow sat back and laughed. "You really think I am that powerful? I can't just call up central bank governors and tell them to close down some of their countries' commercial banks. We haven't even shut down some of our own culprits."

"But you know Mr. Karuhanga. You've often hosted him during his New York visits. Alcoholic, isn't he?"

Winslow shook his head in disbelief. "Can't any of us have some of our own deep secrets? Caleb did partake of the demon drink from time to time. Quit as governor. His Excellency, the president, called him in, gave him hell, and told him to get back to work. Never touched a drop since."

"Wish my pop could have done that. I admire this governor. Would he ever attend the Basle meet?"

"No. There is nothing Caleb would like more, but African central banks are small league. He has often asks me about it in a wistful kind of way."

"Well, please, at least call him. We need help. Terror activity in East Africa is increasing, and we think laundered money is part of the puzzle."

Winslow readjusted a few of his stray curls.

"The global Laundromat for Russian criminal cash is currently in much bigger banks like Denske, Deutsche Bank, RBS, and HSBC. Total of over $80 billion has been washed, dried, and neatly pressed so far. But for terror purposes? It's hard for us to know its use on leaving the Washing Well. Poor Africa if their little banks are getting sucked into this new use of laundering."

"Have you ever visited Africa?'

"Africa? No never been much interested. I prefer my haute cuisine in the Old Ebbitt."

"Your next tome after *Money Matters*, Winslow, needs to be on inequality. I'm sure it's the root cause of all our worries. And it has worsened since the coronavirus outbreak."

Winslow grinned. "I'll get to it right away, Madame Secretary."

Waiters came and went like swooping swallows, and the meal was excellent.

The two childhood sweethearts sat for some time in companionable silence.

The silence was broken by the Secretary's next questions.

"If you want to keep your new job, you need to develop your Basle contacts into wider US and world contacts. Show that you can handle world chaos as well as our local economy. Look, let me test you out. In world affairs, what's our endgame?"

Winslow thought for some time before answering. The answer, if there was one, had serious implications for both of their future careers and the security of ordinary people worldwide.

Winslow chose his words with care.

"Our eyes in the skies are twenty-twenty. Our knowledge of the poverty-stricken hovels and villages on planet earth and the growing army of unemployed young people is confused, to say the least. Inequality is widening daily. Now Abu seems to be working his magic by pulling together many al-Qaeda groups as well as

Islamic State. They have been helped so much by coronavirus without them lifting a finger, and now they must be looking for final body blows against the great Satan, that's us. And look at the mayhem already in East Africa. Abu is also rumored to soon take over from Ayman-al-Zawahiri, the current al-Qaeda leader."

"Very good, Chairman. You are more than just a numbers boy. And post-caliphate and Turkey's invasion of northern Syria, Islamic State is morphing. Funny word, eh? But morphing it is. But into what?"

Winslow sipped his drink. Jeannie's laser eyes met his—ever alert, questioning, focused.

"Go on," she said simply.

"Polarization. That's it. Polarization. What we used to call the Judaeo-Christian world is polarizing into extreme camps. Nationalism with fearful protectionism on the one hand and old socialist ideas on the other. The majority find themselves in a middle ground with no leader. In the world of Islam, there is now a huge rift between extreme Sunni and Shia wings with the majority of Muslims in the middle with no strong leader. Put together the middle people, and you have peace.'

Jeannie clapped her hands. "Bravo, *mon ami*! Bravo!"

Much encouraged, Winslow concluded his thoughts.

"Our war on terror is up against this one strange man. Abu is the glue sticking together al- Shabaab, Islamic State, al-Qaeda, and a string of others in a maelstrom of pure ideological hatred. The coronavirus has already done some of his work weakening the world economy. Now he is looking at a final knock-out punch, coordinating all of them with final orders from Ayman-al-Zawahiri, the Egyptian who replaced bin Laden as the new al-Qaeda chief and whom he may soon replace. So to answer your question, Jeannie, we need to eliminate Abu."

Jeannie smiled, put down her drink, and ran her fingers through her hair. "So refreshing to hear the truth, instead of vote-catching bullshit in the House."

Winslow placed his hand over hers on the table.

The secretary of state quivered but made no move to remove it. "And now we've lost him?"

"Yes. He stopped in Yemen on his way to Somalia to meet with AQAP. AQAP, al-Qaeda in the Arabian Peninsula, is the group most willing to confront us on our home soil. After all, the last three attempted attacks on the US were by AQAP. In a desert location, it seems they have developed a radiological explosive device, the dirty bomb, which is perfect for individual suicide bombers."

"Radioactive! My God!"

Jeannie nodded. "Three large caches of cobalt-60, a metallic substance with lethally high levels of radiation, have been stolen. I won't say from where. We are pretty sure they are now in the hands of Abu and a group of his scientists. Imagine if several of these were set off in key financial districts of New York, London, Frankfurt, Beijing…they could grind the already fragile world economy into sand grains."

"Dear, oh, dear," Winslow muttered lamely. Then he pushed forward toward the Secretary. "Oh God, look, our own American debt is now a staggering twenty-six trillion dollars, which is risky, to say the least. These attacks could nudge us all over the brink."

Jeannie nodded. "We keep hearing one word, *centum*, a kind of terror coalition perhaps of suicide bombers."

"Centum? One hundred?"

"Mmm. That's all I know. Now not a word of this to anyone."

"Deep secrets, Secretary, deep secrets."

The new Chairman (acting) admired the intelligent sparkle in her eyes. Unlike many beltway colleagues, she had more than formidable academic credentials from Princeton, she had street smartness, a realism that came from a family that had also unraveled in front of her childhood eyes. There were times when Winslow felt he could actually see Jeannie's father's drift into alcoholism and despair in her tea-green eyes. The sparkle softened to a kindliness, an inquisitive concern.

"How is your own mother doing, Winslow?" she asked.

What happened next came as a surprise not only to the secretary of state but to the Chairman himself. Winslow Kirk's customary confidence was gone. His Federal Reserve mask slipped. He began to shake uncontrollably.

The maître d' came by to see if he could replenish the drinks. Jeannie shooed him away with a wave of her hand. Jeannie remained totally silent. She placed her small hand on top of Winslow's. Now three hands together. He took a deep breath and looked up. His voice was uncharacteristically low, and Jeannie leant forward to hear more clearly.

"Like many men, I am two distinct people. My public persona and then the nightmare of my own life. Martha Jane died just over a year ago. My own health isn't so good, just completed heart surgery. Coming out of the procedure and since then, I've been having strange dreams, even nightmares, about the boating accident that killed my daughter and lost our granddaughter, Eleanor, to adoption. In each dream I see the little pink teddy I gave her. She would be eighteen by now."

"I think you had better explain, Winslow. Remember everything spoken in Old Ebbitt Bar and Grill here stays right here in Old Ebbitt Bar and Grill."

"Well, you know about the boating disaster when we were caught underwater for God knows how long. My daughter and her husband both died. My wife was ill in hospital after another manic episode. I was in a coma for weeks; came out of it; went into a funk, a deep depression. And Martha Jane had never kept well, and the accident nearly broke her completely. Since I had been at the sailboat helm, Social Services were not convinced that I was fit to adopt. In the middle of all this chaos, I signed over little Eleanor, age three, into adoption. My mother has never forgiven me, and to be honest I have never forgiven myself."

Jeannie nodded but said nothing. The perfect listener.

"I doubled my work rate. Made professor at Yale. Made money through my books, especially *Money Matters*, which is a textbook in many countries. Then I joined the Fed but never quite managed to reach to the top, until today, if what you tell me is true. My father always said that life was just a game of chance, but I worked to prove him wrong. I could control my own destiny. But since then I'm having doubts. Many doubts. Then there's a word I can't get out of my head."

"Sex, maybe?" Jeannie quipped.

Winslow gave a wry grin. "No. *Schuld.*"

"Pardon me?"

"The German Bundesbank president Herr Vogel told us all about it during a visit to the Fed in New York. We were discussing the German demand for austerity in Europe. He is not only a brilliant academic in economics, he also lectures part time in Medieval German literature at Tubingen University."

"A wunderkind?"

"Exactly. He said the word *schuld* has two distinct meanings. In English, we need two words to express this, debt but also shame. This is why Germans often like to rent their houses in case they were to default on a mortgage, which would be extremely shameful."

Jeannie sipped some more wine. "Ask Herr Vogel if it also means alcohol. My father's debt and shame came directly from the bottle."

Winslow replied, "I feel so ashamed of having let Eleanor be adopted, but there's nothing I can do about it now."

The friends were quiet for some time, both wondering about what might have been or maybe still could be.

"Truth is, Jeannie, I find myself in a strange whimsical mood. All my success so far, all my bluster, all my bravado is nothing compared with a deeper need to see Eleanor again. Herr Vogel's word haunts me. My father's debt and my own shame."

Jeannie nodded. "I can understand that. And maybe feel her chubby little hand in yours once more. But, Winslow, the real world beckons. I need your help."

As the friends rose to go, Winston blurted out, "You know what?"

Jeannie shrugged.

As he watched her shoulders rise and fall, he said, "On the way here, I prayed a strange prayer. 'Surprise me Lord.'"

"Well, I hope you find an answer, Winslow. I really do. Would you like to come on by my Adams Morgan apartment?"

Another offer of companionship, intimacy. What had Doris advised? No sex, yet. Little excitement and limited travel. Silence hung between them. A very loud silence. The secretary of state already knew the answer.

Winslow shook his head. "Another time, Jeannie. I'm muddled at the moment in more ways than one. You know I spent a month sleeping in a sofa bed in Martha Jane's hospice room. It's been nearly a year, and memories are surging back. Now I'm muddled, misty even."

"Misty?"

"'My eyes are misty with the affairs of men.' Erdna, the earth goddess in Wagner's marvelous opera *The Ring Cycle*. Martha Jane and I watched part of it in her hospice room for hours before the end."

The childhood sweethearts kissed and went their separate ways into the city of intrigue, Winslow desperately trying to remember what his grandfather had said about answered prayer.

Chapter

3

Teacher Dorcas asked Kiabo to carefully tell her all that had happened in the massacre. They sat together on the verandah of Speke Hotel in Uganda's capital, Kampala, drinking sweet tea and eating meat samosas.

"I need to know everything and hear what you saw."

Kiabo munched her third samosa. This was total luxury. "I wish you were still my teacher," she said. "Why did you leave our lovely Sir Samuel Baker School?"

"Come on, Kiabo, you know why. After your kidnap at Lake Albert, I was so angry. I wanted to help our army security people to keep you and all school children safe. Come on now, the story."

Kiabo sipped her tea and looked out over the neighboring Sheraton Hotel. She stared at the bust of King George V in the Sheraton gardens. For a few brief glorious moments, she was somebody. Somebody who could look out from a hotel instead of looking longingly in.

"Being late for my date saved my life. Well, maybe it wasn't quite a date. But for me it was. My grandmother had delayed me. You know how grandmothers are?"

Dorcas nodded.

"'Have you taken your pills?' she asked me.

'No, Jajja.'

'Here is some water, take them now. You know the nurse told me that they put your AIDS disease in a cage and allow your growing body to work its own miracles.'"

Kiabo stopped speaking.

"Come on, what's wrong?" her ex-teacher encouraged her.

"Teacher Dorcas, I can't forgive these men who took me from Auntie Bella's home in Lake Albert. That's why I have the virus."

Dorcas was now more convinced than ever that her decision to quit teaching and train for Ugandan military intelligence made sense. Security was essential above all else.

"Kiabo, I'm sorry it happened. But your dear brother Ibrahim brought you out. He convinced me to join the army. He told me the whole story. How on the edge of Ituri Forest in DR Congo, he was helped by one of the local pygmies. Kaluki his name was. He spent days with him, and his magic found you, and Ibrahim brought you home. Forgive? I don't know. They are wicked people and should be punished. But please go on."

"Grandma then sent me to Mama Kellen at her little *duka* to pay off her month's debt of Uganda shillings 50,000, about $15, covering sugar, kerosene, millet flour, matches, combination artemesia malaria medicine for my little sister Naomi, and two phone calls on Kellen's Nokia phone. The money had come as usual from my older brother Caleb, same mother, same father, who is training to be a plumber. He sent it regularly. I then worried that sweat from such a rush now would spoil my new hairstyle called score. You know how these things can worry you so much?"

Dorcas smiled. "In my army training, my hairstyle was pretty messed up at times."

"You see, it was a date, but on the other hand, it wasn't. I had spent hours having my hair braided in one of the latest styles, so yes, it was a date. My younger sister Naomi, same mother same father, earns a few shillings on weekends sweeping and cleaning in Last Chance Salon and had borrowed a poster showing all the latest styles This now hangs proudly on the plaster-peeling wall of Granny's room. Copying the poster and replicating the intricate twists and turns, pulling and kneading of the stylists, she did a great job on my hair. I wore blue jeans and whitish T-shirt, and honestly, I thought I looked great. I am so thin, so the jeans gripped my waist real tight. Since Granny is ever broke, it keeps me thin. You know how bright butterfly wings flip? Well, my heart was like that. Bright-purple jacaranda flowers formed a perfect ground cover carpet for a first date. The night was balmy. A breath of freshness drifted from Lake Victoria over the great airport town of Entebbe. On the other hand, it wasn't a date. My older brother Alano, same mother different father, had a few days leave and had told me that he was planning to watch the final of the soccer World Cup in Tarzan Garden's large outdoor screens in Entebbe with his chum Albert. Even when I heard his name, my heart had flipped, like one of Granny's chicks when you step near them. Well, I asked if I could join them. I took my brother's 'why not' shrug as a firm invite, and well, here I was. I pushed forward through rows of white plastic chairs. On one of the side screens, I watched a spectacular save from a goalkeeper and smiled at the groan of the crowd. My one-size too-small used sneakers—a gift from Auntie Bellain, who lives in an island in Lake Albert, she could never keep up with my growing, you see—knocked over several Bell beer bottles lying on the grass. I ignored the protests and abuse from boys and men and pushed on. Then I spotted them in the front row. 'Albert!' He turned and smiled, waving for me to join them. I smiled back. Maybe it was a date after all."

Dorcas thought of her own romance and its dissolution when she left teaching.

"But then I decided to go back to the bar and bring Albert a beer. This saved me. As I walked back to the bar, I saw a flash of bright light and watched in horror as my brother Alano and Albert and many more young people rose into the air. I put my hands over my ears as a deafening explosion followed. I fell backward and landed on top of those still sitting, and together we crashed down onto the grass. Chaos ensued. Voices screamed around us. 'Run! Al-Shabaab! Get out!' they yelled. As we lay on the grass, a boy beside me switched on his mobile phone, which lit up. It illumined the face of a thin brown man who was stepping over us all to get out. Somali maybe. I saw him like a photo, then he was gone."

"This man, would you recognize him again?" Dorcas asked.

"I think so, Teacher."

Kaibo continued with her story.

*****

Then in some bizarre twist of fate, the screens kept showing the game. A professional foul was committed, and the referee pointed to the penalty spot. Then someone tripped over the wiring, and all together the screens went out. Like the lives of my brother Alano and Albert and so many other young people that evening, the match was over before halftime. An eternity later, among medics and paramedics and nurses and ambulances, I found the mangled, broken, bloody remains of my brother and my date. A hand touched my shoulder, gentle as a spider's web.

"Don't touch. Go home. Bodies can be identified tomorrow in Mulago Hospital morgue," the nurse said and then hugged me. That hug will stay with me for a lifetime.

I walked home in a numbness that was almost comforting. But still I did not want to reach home. How could I tell Granny that Alano was dead? How could I even face Granny? A half-moon bowed behind a cloud, and I was glad of the ensuing total darkness. I now asked myself the question that was rarely far from my mind, but tonight it took on an urgency I had never known before. Why is there so much suffering in the world? I turned a corner and was blinded by an overhead light surrounded by flying ants, which sizzled and then dropped onto a corrugated iron chute and on into a forty-gallon drum. Entebbe's protein for the next day. As I blinked, I saw clearly my mother's face as she sold these delicacies, fried and salted, in the market. Yes, my suffering had begun then, that moment when Mother grew thinner and thinner and then she was no more. Granny took over the flying-ants business. I moved silently toward the little one-room house, which was home to

Granny; myself; Alano; and Naomi, my little sister. Pushing open the door, I was startled to hear my grandmother's voice behind me coming from the *shamba*.

"Kiabo?"

"Yes, Jajja."

I shivered as I turned toward the cassava patch. The old woman pushed her five-foot frame up and then sat down again. In that moment I saw how much smaller and slower she now seemed. She sat in her flower-patterned nightdress, which, when newer, she had even worn to the little local church. It had seen many washings, and the red flowers were light pink. When she spoke again, her voice was weak as a faraway cricket's croak. But even in the darkness, I could see those penetrating eyes in her black gnarled face as she leaned forward.

"Mama Kellen at the duka came by. She told me about the explosion. Her radio was speaking about it. Some deep whisper inside me, maybe from my granny's spirit, told me there was evil. Alano?"

"Granny, Alano is dead."

Granny put her face into her rough work-worn hands and began to shake. I looked up. The half-moon reappeared, and a few stars sparkled dimly. An owl hooted from a guava tree branch just above a small enclosure containing Granny's two pink piglets and four charms, one at each corner, to repel thieves.

"Alano. He was a good boy. A great goalkeeper for his team and would have been a good plumber. With his small wages, he paid off Mama Kellen every month."

My spirits plunged deeper. These other implications of Alano's death were now dawning on me. Now that I had finished high school, my dream of beginning nursing training was over. I would have to find a job, any job, to support Granny and Naomi. I looked up, and Granny was standing in front of me.

"Come, girl, come," she said, and I allowed her to hold me very tight, much tighter than the nurse's embrace.

"Jajja, it was terrible. I saw them in the front row and walked toward them."

Granny allowed me to recall and retell the horrible moment just as I am telling you now.

We were quiet for some time. Little Naomi emerged from the one-room house. I looked into my little sister's face, so thin, so gray and pale after the fever.

"I have to fix the holes in the mosquito netting," I told myself.

"What's wrong?" Naomi asked.

"Everything, Naomi," I whispered. "Everything is wrong."

Then Granny, ever practical, spoke again. "The funeral. We need money for the funeral.

Even the price of bark cloth has gone up."

"Death itself is the only free thing on earth, but for those of us left behind, it's expensive," I replied.

"Teacher Dorcas. She left your school nearly a year ago. I never understood why," Granny said.

"I'll go to Mama Kellen's and use her pig's ear," I said. "You know, her Nokia phone."

"You know her number?" Jajja asked.

I touched my head.

"It is now the one thing that will save us all, Kiabo, your brains. God gave you them, and your mother left you a lovely name, Kiabo, the gift. Her gift, now my gift. And tell Mama Kellen to come back with a bottle of Uganda *waragi* gin, put it on my slate. We all need to weep."

Mama Kellen arrived, and other neighbors drifted in. Entebbe was a restless town, and sleep seemed far from anyone's thoughts. Naomi, still in a daze, heard the news in fits and starts from many neighbors and collapsed in a heap. I picked her up and held her tight. She had always been so much weaker than me, and since Mommy died, I had always to care for her. Tonight she seemed so small, so vulnerable. She looked moon gray rather than black. Through the ululations, cries and groans, prayers to the Lord of us all, Granny took me aside. We walked together into the little *shamba* where the new variety disease-free cassava was almost ready for harvesting.

"Teacher Dorcas?"

"Jajja, she sends her greetings and says she is so very sorry about Alano. Her driver will come tomorrow with some cash for the funeral expenses."

"She is a good woman, your very best English teacher. What is she doing now?"

I shrugged. Then for the second time that night, I was hugged, but much more tightly than the nurse's hug. I could feel every one of Granny's bones sticking into me.

"Kiabo, the gift, thank God for you. You must help us all," Granny said.

I held her tighter.

*****

Kiabo noticed that one lonely meat samosa was lingering on the plate, and she picked it up and munched into it.

"Teacher Dorcas, thank you. You helped us so much with the funeral."

"Least I could do, Kiabo. But go on please. You are telling it well."

"Well, that's it, Teacher. Somehow, despite my own deep misgivings, I managed the next few words in Granny's ear. 'You, dear Jajja, will play till full time, I promise you.'"

Dorcas paid the bill. Then Kiabo asked the question she was afraid to ask.

"Ibrahim?" Her brother. Same mother different father, a Muslim father.

"I'm sorry, we don't know, Kiabo. On our latest peacekeeping mission to Somalia, he was captured by al-Shabaab. We don't know any more."

"He saved me. You must get him back, please."

"We are doing everything, I promise you."

"Oh, suppose you will now cancel our Camp Hopeful after this bombing?"

"No, Kiabo, it will go ahead. And by the way, you've reminded me. The American lady who has been helping with your school fees died recently, as you know. Well, I received a message that her daughter is coming over to camp. I want you to show her round and bring her up to our second Camp Hopeful."

Kiabo nodded. As Teacher Dorcas rose to leave, Kiabo followed her, glancing back for one last lingering look at the lovely Speke Hotel.

Chapter

4

Some people think that the president of the United States is the most powerful person in the world. Jeannie Backhouse knew differently. This morning she chose to enter her work through Washington's main C Street entrance. She needed time to reflect on all that was happening. She was grateful that she had been able to call her mother in Maine, firming up a visit. She was now focused on discussions with her lawyer on the terms for her divorce and an Africa trip with several senators, which she had postponed. She paused after entering the main hall and stood respectfully beside the wall as she read the names of all Foreign Service officers killed in the line of duty between 1780 and 2002. During that time, 83 had been lost in the first 187 years, and 126 in the subsequent 35 years.

The State Department plaque clearly reflected more simple times, she thought. Today the losses per year are nine times as great as in these previous times, she reminded herself. My job is to make sure there are no more, certainly not on my watch and now there was this potential threat in East Africa.

Leaving the crowd of worker ants in their respective cubes behind her, Jeannie then used her pass to take the private elevator to the seventh floor. In the ornate-paneled hallway, she stared at some of her predecessors. Portraits of Jefferson, Marshal, Rice, Schultz, Albright (who understood suffering), Clinton, Kerry met her steady gaze. She had only held the secretary of state position for less than a year, and already she felt the burden heavy on her shoulders. She looked into the huge state room used for ceremonial visits and once again paused as if to draw inspiration from the setting. She loved the dazzling collection of eighteenth-century furniture and paintings, but her favorite piece was Thomas Jefferson's grandfather clock right beside her in the doorway. It kept perfect time, and for her was the best symbol of continuity over the years. As she neared her smaller office, a few staff, a new intern, seemed to sense her tension and huddled in a protective laager round the Poland Spring water cooler. She pushed open her office door and yelled, "Tami!"

Her PA winked at her colleagues at the water cooler and followed the Secretary into her office.

"Close the door, please," she said.

Her assistant remained standing as Jeannie slipped into a chair behind her huge ornate mahogany desk, the desk that had been her grandfather's when he was a senator. Another grandfather clock stood in the corner, one that had been in her family for generations. To some extent she was living up to her grandfather but also doing all this for her father who had left life too early. Like Jefferson's, the clock also kept perfect time. Jeannie's tiny frame was dwarfed in the generous chair. Her family motto had always been the biblical "Not to be ministered unto but to minister," and in her current position, she gave 100 plus percent and drove her subordinates very hard. She was willing to sacrifice her personal life and her health for the cause, but now some crumbs of doubt were dropping in. Some admired her, but few could claim to know or like her.

"Sit, Tami. We have a situation. Try to get me Ambassador Jimmy Marsh on the phone. You know our man in Uganda. I don't care if he's drinking, playing, snoozing, eating, or even working. I need him now!"

A short time later Jeannie was connected to her ambassador in Uganda. She indicated to Tamsin to leave her.

"Jimmy, security level in East Africa is now high." No foreplay, no preliminaries. "When I sent you out there, I told you, 'No body bags.' I still mean it. None at all, you hear me! No Americans died in the Entebbe bombing, but many Ugandan young people and some Europeans did."

Ambassador Marsh muttered assent.

"We missed Abu in the recent strike in Somalia, but we've stirred up a hornet's nest. There have been messages from Shura, you know, the think tank behind al-Qaeda and affiliate terror groups to al-Shabaab. We think they have already established safe havens in Uganda or adjoining countries for the European, Middle Eastern, and other al-Qaeda recruits who have now slipped out of Iraq, and the Islamic State fellows who have recently escaped out of northeast Syria. Try to find any safe havens for terror cells. Use any sources you can find. What backup do you have on hand now?"

Jimmy Marsh poured himself another Jack Daniels. The ice from his previous drink had melted, and he plopped in a couple of fresh ice blocks, trying not to make any sound into his iPhone.

"We do have a Tilt rotor CV-22 Osprey right here in Entebbe, ma'am."

Ambassador Marsh was referring to the most sophisticated aircraft, designed after the failure of the Iran hostage rescue mission in 1980.The CV-22 tilt rotor Osprey could take off and land vertically and carry combat troops.

"It has its own crew here. They've just dropped off four of our Delta boys in Juba, Southern Sudan, to rehearse a possible evacuation of the embassy staff and perhaps the NGO staff from there." The ambassador was referring to the elite army unit Delta Force. "Should we ask them to return to Entebbe?"

"No, Jimmy. What they are preparing for is vital. Evacuation from Juba, South Sudan, could be imminent. Still nice to know they are close by."

"I also, of course, have our new defense attaché, Wallace Willard."

Given the recent rise in terror activity in the region, Willard was new and was himself a Marine.

"I have heard in the last few hours that Abu may have moved from Somalia to Kenya or even Uganda. Can't imagine why, but there you are."

"Terrorists, like God, work in mysterious ways, ma'am," Jimmy replied. "Their wonders to perform."

"You're getting too cynical in your old age, Ambassador. This may be your last posting, but for God's sake, make the most of it. We are extending our travel advisory beyond Southern Sudan to include Uganda and Kenya. Keep me informed of all, and I mean all, developments."

The ambassador asked himself why this final posting was turning out to be so eventful instead of golf and a few innocuous diplomatic chats.

The Secretary sipped some more of her Ugandan Sipi Falls coffee and put her mug down. The mug had been given to her by her pastor years ago as a wedding present. It said simply, "Prayer. God's Social Network." She stared into space.

Jimmy's stomach muscles tightened. He tried to relax and imagine himself sailing in a forty-seven-foot chartered catamaran into the coral-crusted island of Anegada in the British Virgin Isles, but such retirement pursuits now seemed light years away.

"And your visit, Madame Secretary?"

"Don't know yet. As you know I postponed it due to the bombings and then my mother's ill health. Now some of the senators who were to come with me don't want to miss the Correspondents Dinner with the president, which is coming up tomorrow evening. So nothing definite yet."

"Yes, ma'am," the ambassador said. To himself, he said, "God, the Correspondents Dinner, yes, that's more important than the expansion of every terror network we know and some!"

"I know what you're thinking, Jimmy. Desk people in comfort in D. C. and you in the frontline. It's not that simple, and you know it. You try telling President Kamala each twist and calamity turn in this crazy world on the skids. She's beginning to call me Calamity Jean! Don't forget I spent a couple of years in Uganda with Peace Corps. Taught some great kids and have kept in touch with a few."

"Yes, ma'am," the ambassador replied. "Never knew you were clairvoyant, ma'am."

"Part of the essential qualifications for this job, you know. And keep an eye on our folks who are working there now. Make sure they know about the travel advisory so that few new arrivals come in."

"Guests are already here, Jimmy. Serve up some drinks, would you!"

Ambassador Jimmy held his hand over the phone until his wife stopped shouting.

"Apologies, Madame Secretary, I am being called out on urgent business."

The secretary of state stood up as she uttered the next words.

"Nothing, Ambassador, absolutely nothing is more important or urgent than your close liaison with me and my team. Understood!"

Jimmy muttered consent and gratefully said good-bye to his boss.

At the dinner that evening, Ambassador Jimmy found himself obsessed with the White House Correspondents Association Dinner. When his evening guests were seated, he stood up and began addressing them.

"Imagine for a minute that we are now in Washington Hilton Hotel. Tonight we are all in black tie and slinky revealing dresses ready for the occasion. You are now stepping into the hotel's magnificent setting. This will be special for each of us, a heady evening, from the flower arrangements to the exquisite Californian and French wines, not to mention all the beautiful celebs. By the way, this is the real event and not just the pre and post parties that seemed to extend long before and after the dinner itself. Together we look out over the sparkling glitterati of media, money, and politics. For an evening, please forget about the harsh reality of folks' lives outside and certainly very far away from many Ugandans who are wondering where their next meal is coming from. Our table as you can see is beside the top table of the president and her media and business guests."

Jimmy took a long swig of red wine and then continued.

"So welcome old chums to the cabaret, welcome to the media, money, political circus. From the dizzy heights of a tightrope stunt in Senate/Congress, even White House high office, you can then do well as a lobbyist clown within this fairy-tale nation's capital where reality and fantasy join hands in an orgy of opulence. Welcome to the town, our town, that puts the 'me' into media!"

The guests clapped and laughed. Jimmy's wife, Gloria, rolled her eyes and muttered to the guest beside her, "Thank God he's retiring soon before he's fired!"

Little did she know just how eventful her husband's final weeks before retirement were to be.

*****

Winslow Kirk pushed both his hands through his mop of curls.

"Chairman Kirk is here now, Madame Secretary," Tami relayed the message, held the door open for Winslow, and retreated to safer ground. Things were now hotter than she had ever experienced in her four years in this position.

"Come in, Winslow, come in. And help yourself to great Ugandan coffee."

Winslow poured himself a cup and added a splash of milk.

"I love that word you used at our dinner, Jeannie. What was it? Unraveling? That's it. Our world is unraveling before our eyes, and we are impotent observers."

He stood looking at the grandfather clock ticking rhythmically in the corner of the Secretary's office.

"Sit down for goodness sake. Let me get a coffee refill," Jeannie said.

"I understand the situation in Uganda is much worse?"

Jeannie nodded. "Our intelligence isn't great, but yes, it seems that Abu has left Somalia and is actually in Kenya or Uganda now. We don't know why since it is a big risk for him. He must have serious safe havens he can use."

"But why?"

"Why anything! Tyrants and logic don't exactly mix. You remember what Thomas Jefferson suggested for the American motto?"

"No. Only an aspiring presidential candidate would know that."

"Rebellion to tyrants is obedience to God."

"Thanks, Jeannie. Just· what I need. Some useless philosophizing!"

"Look, the president wants to know if we should evacuate our embassy staff in Kampala."

Winslow sipped his coffee.

"Your call. Thank God I just do numbers. They don't talk or throw bombs! Abu is unique to say the least. He has also begun sending out very direct social media hate messages. He seems to work with a very small elite group."

Jeannie poured herself some more coffee.

"His hate messages and the hate messages some of our political leaders are putting out are just making our lives more complex. They put in danger the lives of our overseas folks."

"Nonbiodegradable," Winslow muttered.

"Pardon me?"

"I said nonbiodegradable. An expression used by, I believe, by retired Gen. David Petraeus. The hate words uttered by terror groups or by our own politicians enter our body politic and never leave."

The secretary of state smiled. "So true, Winslow, so true." The Secretary returned to the imminent threat. "Doesn't make sense to me. Why does Abu risk taking his elite group into the lion's den of Kenya or Uganda?"

"I think it's linked to our recent strike, which clearly missed him."

Winslow looked back at the clock. *Tick, tick, tick...*

"You know until the recent rise of ISIS, Islamic State, al-Shabaab controlled more territory than any other Qaeda subgroup. I do believe we now have them on the run, but this development in Kenya and Uganda is strange and, frankly, has me worried. But evacuate? No, I don't think so. Excellent coffee by the way."

"It's Ugandan Arabica from Mount Elgon. It's called Sipi Falls after the waterfall from the mountain. A small group of farmers are now marketing it in some high-end supermarkets and Starbucks."

"It's strong. And the flavor is mango, earthy, unique."

"Have you spoken to Caleb Karuhanga in Kampala yet?"

"For two seconds. He was boarding a flight back to Entebbe from Dar es Salaam. We agreed to talk soon."

The two childhood sweethearts stared at each other. Carefully balancing her coffee, Jeannie reached over and brushed her lips against Winslow's cheek, still wondering what might have been or even what might still be. The grandfather clock continued its rhythmic ticking. Winslow opened his mouth to speak.

"Urgent call, Secretary, from Uganda." The PA Tamsin stuck her head round the door.

"Get out, Tami, we're busy!" Jeannie snapped. "Tell Jimmy I'll call him back."

Clearly disappointed that a kind of special moment between them had passed, the secretary of state was now wondering about another important part of her life.

Her PA, however, did not retreat. "Madam Secretary, it is not the ambassador. It's the Ugandan president."

Winslow stood up. "Jeannie, I'll be outside in the visitor's room. We can talk after the call."

Tami carried his coffee out and brought him a glass of water.

"Never seen the Secretary snap like that before. Sure, she has a temper, but she keeps telling me to alert her to any urgent communications."

Winslow shrugged. "Lot going on at the moment," he murmured. "An awful lot."

Tami couldn't possibly disagree as she noticed a smear of pink lipstick on the visitor's cheek.

As he sipped his coffee, Winston mused over some thoughts for his latest book on inequality, *The Market as Servant*.

Needs a more sexy title, he thought.

The market place must be the servant of our dreams, not the master. A more equitable market place is not impossible. Never in history has people's reality been so affected by systems created by so few. But as ever, his mind returned to the sea. Each bubble of milk in the coffee mug became a wave. He became mesmerized and began muttering to himself.

"Wing to wing. Mainsail port, jib starboard. I began to push the tiller for our jibe. Sheets were extended correctly. Suddenly a weird and sudden wind shift. We jibed prematurely. The whiplash of the boom skimmed my head, which would explain the later coma. The wind increased and pushed the sailboat over. All of us landed in the Sound. The Nor'easter came out of nowhere and pummeled the waves. Why didn't I see it coming?

"The morning had begun so beautifully. Daughter Zephyr had prepared coffee and her famous lax of bagels, salmon, and cream cheese. It was a glorious autumn morning. As we motored out from our slip into the channel, we admired the shoreline of myriad colors. Flurries of yellow and russet and brown leaves caressed the shore. As we raised the mainsail, Zephyr made the announcement. 'Now is as good a time as any,' she said. 'I'm pregnant.' 'Martha Jane will be so happy, and Eleanor will have a new brother or sister.' 'Raise the jib,' said Russ. 'This sail is a perfect lullaby for the wee one.'

"All of this joy and family anticipation of expansion crashed to an end as the boom smashed Zephyr's head as *Currentcy* keeled over and hit the waves.

"My grandfather's lessons in underwater swimming and breath control for long periods in St. Andrews helped me but not the others. I was blind semiconscious underwater and useless to help. As the storm developed, the sea became darker and darker. I alone survived. Why?"

There was no reply from the coffee mug.

"Come on in, Buttsy," the secretary of state yelled as she edged the door open a crack. "Enjoy the coffee?"

Winston shook his head to return to the real world. "Excellent. Yes, I love it. So what's up?"

Jeannie Backhouse slumped into the softest of the scarlet sofas beside Winslow. "Bad, Winslow, real bad."

Winslow raised his bushy eyebrows inquisitively but allowed time for the Secretary to continue. The clock's ticking seemed louder than usual. Outside the room, silence reigned as Tami shooed her colleagues away from the cooler.

"The Ugandan president has just arrested some Somalis who were obviously running a test with their dirty bomb, the radiological dispersion device, in a large shopping mall in Kololo. You know they also prevented the bombing of the third US Embassy in 1998 when Nairobi and Dar es Salaam were hit. The Ugandans are brilliant at intel and security on the ground."

Winslow put his coffee mug down and stared at the grandfather clock mimicking a ticking bomb. "Shit! Is this really happening?"

"I'm sending a team in right away to find out what we can about the explosives used and how they were concealed."

Jeannie stood up and began pacing the room.

"The team can do their work. It's likely the radiological dispersion device is being perfected in a factory in rural Yemen."

"Doesn't make our anti-terror equipment look too good," Winslow said.

"Damn right, it doesn't," Jeannie muttered before continuing. "The Ugandan president spoke again about the real possibility of Abu actually being in Uganda and using safe havens in the country or neighboring Congo. As you know, Kenyan and Ugandan troops have been superb helping the fight against al-Shabaab in Somalia. The president reminded me for the umpteenth time that his soldiers are our boots on the ground in Somalia and asked me why his poor little country was being punished like this and why the hell Abu is making a journey to the heart of Africa. He was in full flow and reminded me that his little country is now hosting over one million refugees from South Sudan and Congo in northern camps."

"Journey to the Heart." Winslow blinked and sucked in some breath.

"What?" Jeannie asked.

"Journey to the Heart. Oh, nothing, just something my mother was talking about. A screenplay. She has too much time on her hands and gets sidetracked easily with nonsense."

The secretary of state stood up abruptly, bringing their meeting to an end.

But Winslow wasn't leaving without confirmation of his promotion.

"Chairman?" he said simply. "Everyone seems to think I'm chairman of the Federal Reserve System except me."

"Sorry, Winslow, sorry. Look you will hear from the treasury secretary in the next hour, and yes, you will be going to Basle to represent them in a couple of days. I know you've always dreamed of that."

"What about Elwood?"

"He's had a relapse, I'm afraid. Seemed to be doing well after his Covid-19 treatment, but now he is isolated again."

"I'm sorry to hear that. Thought it was all over. Will this damn corona virus ever leave us in peace?"

"He is back on leave. And, Winslow, I hope you are looking after yourself. We need fit troops at this time."

"Yes, ma'am," the new Fed Chairman (acting, acting) muttered.

"It's probably too late, Winslow. But please, please try to plug the Pearl of Africa Bank cash transfers for terror purposes."

"Promise."

"And when you are in Basle, put pressure to stop laundering especially if it is used for terror purposes."

Winslow suddenly saw the two of them somersaulting down sand dunes on Block Island. Happier times. Simpler times. He saw Jeannie's carefree curls twirling in the sand dunes. *Why couldn't life just stay that way?* he wondered wistfully. Little did he know just how far he was about to sail into more dark, dangerous, and turbulent waters.

Chapter

5

Home again by the sea. The sea that took his father. The sea that took his son-in-law and daughter and, as a result after her adoption, his granddaughter. The cruel sea.

"I leave for Basle early tomorrow, Mother."

"I thought you were told no excitement and limited travel?"

"Just a brief visit, and then I need to be back to chair the Fed in two days' time. This is such a fabulous opportunity. Just when I thought retirement was imminent." Winslow stopped speaking as he saw his mother's lips tremble. A few tears trickled down her cheeks. "What's wrong?" He walked over, hugged his mother, and sat down beside her.

"When you were in D. C. I've been going through these old papers you helped bring down from the attic. Some of your father's writing and some old sermons of your grandfather. I came across a paper your father had written and put in a file describing in detail how the final financial collapse actually happened." She handed it over to Winslow. "Seems we were destroyed by a seagull's wing."

Winslow sat down. He was concerned that of late his mother was not just forgetful but sometimes incoherent. The carers shared some of the stories with him.

"Don't be ridiculous, Mother. He just lost in a golf game, that's all."

"Read it out to me. I need to hear the truth, every rotten, hellish detail."

Winslow shrugged.

"As you wish, Mother," he sighed. He took the papers in his hand, papers his father had prepared after his visit to Scotland. *Strange, none of us have seen this before*, he thought.

*****

All yellow. Dandelions, buttercups, and yellow gorse on the hills surrounding the City and Royal Burgh of St. Andrews. Here in the home of golf I had one chance to reverse my fortunes. Double or quit. Boom or bust. Jack Aasen and I had the same handicap. Jack now held the title deeds of our home were I to lose. If I won I owed him nothing. I would be free of my gambling debt. A cool, light east wind, a gossamer *haar*, the locals call it, blew off the Firth of Forth. My ivory golf pants and short-sleeved light-blue shirt fitted just right. I looked down at the fabled Old Course with her sand dunes clinging protectively round her. I thought of my father and his ideas of heaven. Mine were different. For me this was heaven…if I won.

Jack is the founder and chief executive of Myfans, the biggest of America's latest financial fads. I don't pretend to understand all the ins and outs of it, but basically, they inaugurate initial public offerings for athletes buying a percent of an athlete's estimated future earnings and selling investors shares stock linked to actual economic performance. I suppose this no different from what we are about to do now—bet on each other's sporting performance.

My partner was a Scot, Alec McNab, who knew the course well. Jack's partner was Khalil, a basketball player who played for the Detroit Nets. He had arrived in Minnesota as a kid from Somalia, was now a citizen, and had experienced the American Dream in spades. He was over six foot eight, fast and accurate, with an incredible ability to score consistently. Only twenty-two years old, Khalil led most players in Player Efficiency Rating (a per-minute statistic aimed at illustrating a player's overall value), and although he himself did not know this, he was being aggressively targeted by Jack to sign up as one of his sportsmen clients since Jack was sure that Khalil's future earnings were potentially huge. Our playing partners knew nothing of our bet.

The wind was ever shifting but mainly from the North Sea from the east. By the eighteenth hole, I was one stroke behind. My third shot bounced off the arched gray stonework of the thousand-year-old Swilcan Bridge over the Swilcan Burn and ran along the fairway onto the huge green facing the Royal and Ancient Club House. Jack's third missed the bridge and ran to within a mere eight feet of the hole. I took two puts to finish, and now Jack needed to hole this put in order to win the match. Several tourists watched from the front of the club house unaware of the huge stakes. Jack and I never looked at each other. Our partners finished their round and respectfully stood back to allow Jack to put, just eight feet away from my house disappearing. Jack pushed back his shoulders and moved them round in circular fashion. He tried to steady his hands as he addressed the ball with the putter. Taking a very deep silent breath, he gently hit the ball. It moved obediently over the green. My heart stopped. My lungs stopped pushing air in and out. Even the seagulls now seemed to be silent. Nothing moved. It was dead center and traveled straight to the hole. Jack looked at me in triumph, then returned his gaze to the ball. The white Titleist slowed as it reached the cusp of the hole, and then inexplicably, it stopped. I allowed myself one tentative breath. I had won. My house was safe. I could face Eleanor again. Frozen in time, Jack stared at the ball. His caddie shook his head in disbelief.

"Bad luck, Jack, so close," I whispered.

Still Jack did not move, his face ashen.

It seemed an eternity, but in fact only five seconds passed. Just then a seagull took off from the Silcan Bridge and swooped over the eighteenth green. With a scream, it dived for the little white object nestling there. Perhaps a delicious egg. The first swoop was merely an investigation and the long white wing tipped the ball as the seagull made a fly-past. The ball plopped into the hole.

*****

"You see, a seagull's wing destroyed us," Eleanor whispered. "But go on."

"I'm beginning to understand your forgiveness being so tough," Winslow murmured. He read on.

*****

Jack grinned. "I've won," he said hopefully.

"That's a cheat, doesn't count," I yelled.

My partner, Rob McNab, took control. "Well, gentlemen, we'll have to consult the committee in the Club House, but my understanding is that two rules apply here. One is that the movement of the ball by fox, badger, bird can happen and the ball must be left where moved by the animal. The second is the ten-second rule."

"What the hell is that!" I screamed.

My home was disappearing one more time.

"If a ball is poised on the cusp of the hole, and within a period of ten seconds drops into the hole, then the shot counts. This clearly happened within a ten-second period."

I was not convinced, and we all made our way into the Club House. Several members of the Royal and Ancient were called from their post liquid-lunch slumbers in worn brown leather chairs. They listened carefully to the situation, checked with the other two players that a period of more than ten seconds had not elapsed, and then declared that Jack's putt counted. They solemnly confirmed in writing the four score cards for the round.

I cannot face Eleanor. That night I drank heavily in Kate Kennedy pub. The evening was warm. A soft evening the Scots call it. Church bells were ringing. What did Eleanor tell me what John Donne wrote, "Ask not for whom the bell tolls it tolls for thee." Thee that is me, Winston Kirk. A poster outside the pub explained that Kate had been the niece of Bishop Kennedy, Bishop of St. Andrews. She was very beautiful, popular with the students, and every year when she visited in the spring church bells would ring. The bell of St. Salvator's College cast in Paris bears this inscription. "That holy man, James Kennedy, bishop of St. Andrews and founder of the College of the Holy Saviour, had me cast in the year 1460, giving me the name Katherine." The University Kate Kennedy Club, a very select all-male society selected a first-year male student, a bejant, to play the role of Kate in the Club's annual historic pageant through the streets of St. Andrews. I drank in the history since my own life was near its end. I knew then that my life on this earth was over. That John Donne quote that Eleanor loved went over and over in my mind. "Ask not for whom the bell tolls, it tolls for thee."

*****

"Bastard!" Eleanor muttered. "Bastard! He destroyed us."

"And you rebuilt us, Mother. Thank you."

"I hate golf."

"Oh, come on, nothing wrong with the game. It's quite an intellectual pursuit, you know. I do my best thinking on the golf course."

"An intellectual pursuit, eh? In that case women are much better at it than men."

"Why?"

"Men are not good at putting their brains before their balls."

"Oh, Mother! Dad had a serious addiction far worse than nicotine or booze. I think he was just wired that way. 'Life, a game of chance,' he always said."

Eleanor nodded. "Maybe it is, Win. Maybe it is."

"Grandpa didn't think so. I remember him in the streets of Duddingston, funny how all this is coming back to me, yelling at a parishioner. The young man told him that he got a new job just after his prayers in church. 'What a coincidence,' he told Grandpa. Grandpa yelled, 'If you think that's a coincidence, I wish you a very dull life! The very hand of God, lad, the very hand of God.'"

*****

As he went off to pack, Winslow saw his mother sitting morose and muttering, "A seagull's wing, a seagull's wing."

In his carry-on hand luggage, Winslow found some of the papers his mother had been talking about, which she had put there. Some of his grandfather's sermons and a strange old book with his grandfather's surname as author—*The Secret Commonwealth of Elves, Fauns and Fairies* by Robert Kirk.

He went back to ask his mother about it.

"You're making me overweight with all this paperwork. Did Grandpa write this?"

Eleanor smiled.

"No, he wasn't that old. This was written in 1690. After your grandfather's funeral, I found it in a wonderful old secondhand bookshop in West Port Edinburgh, musty, huge rickety ladders to help you reach the high shelves. I loved it and spent hours there, quite comforting in its way after your grandfather's death. Anyway, it is his surname and the author was a minister. He was the seventh son and clearly had the second sight himself. This book is full of stories backing up the second sight. I wonder if he was a relative of his."

"Well, you can work on ancestry while I'm away. This is going to look very odd among my finance, bank, and numbers tomes. Imagine *Money Matters* alongside *The Secret Commonwealth of Elves, Fauns and Fairies!*"

Eleanor smiled. "Look after yourself, lad, you've all I've left. Come back quick and safe."

"You've all I've left." Winslow felt a powerful sense of responsibility for her. The woman who had rebuilt their lives from nothing. The woman who had scrimped and saved so that he could be educated. Everything had gone so well until the second catastrophe, a wind change.

Back at his packing, Winslow saw himself during a soft summer evening in the manse garden in Duddingston Village, Edinburgh.

As close to contentment as you could imagine. His grandmother brought scones straight from the oven, and she lathered on butter and some of her raspberry jam made from the manse raspberry bushes. His grandfather seemed to be becoming more forgetful and often repeated stories. Or was it just a ruse to encourage his grandmother to poke fun.

"Imagine it was in this very garden that…"

Grannie and Winslow would always reply before he could finish. "That Sir Walter Scott wrote *The Heart of Midlothian.*"

"Sir Walter Scott went to my school, don't you know? Royal High School."

They sat on green wooden benches under what Grampa called The Mantle, a trellis with climbing roses encircling it. Other larger rosebushes around it. Peace was his favorite, yellow with salmon-pink fringes. And the scent, intoxicating. Bees also appreciated The Mantle, and the contentment was often serenaded by their loud bee busyness.

Such memory. As the mollusk forms in the oyster, a protecting layer slowly covers the mollusk's organs. A mantle, it's called. Was Winslow's memory forming this mantle round his incipient pearl of mystery?

Chapter

6

Her apartment was chaos but cheerful day-after chaos. The large 5 and 0 candles were now part of the debris Willow Carr swept up. Music, dancing, jokes, laughter, beer, wine, and some great catered bites; but now here she was once again alone. She thought of the article she had read a few days ago in the *New Yorker*, "Loneliness – the rich world's new scourge." Somehow the big 5-0 made it worse. She had already been awake since the wee hours. Somehow deep uninterrupted sleep seemed so elusive. Of course, she thought too much about everything she knew that it was part of her problem. Willow spooned some coffee into the maker and ran through her packing checklist. On the kitchen table, she saw a hurriedly written note.

"Don't know what you are missing. Love, Jim."

Jim. She had said no and good night. She wanted a more permanent relationship, maybe even marriage again, but if not that, at least a solid, steady friendship. She checked her passport, boarding pass and e-ticket. Truth be told, she was now doubting herself and her own motivation for the work she did. Just over a year ago she had suggested the idea of a camp get together for some of the HIV-positive young people she worked with in Uganda. First camp had been super successful and well-funded, especially a generous donation from the wife of a movie mogul. Now she was heading for the second camp a year later. But now she asked herself was it just something to make up for her own missing child. The missing boy Robert, dear Bobby, who had died age three. Bobby, whose absurd death—her fault really, wasn't it?—led to the final disintegration of a marriage. After all this, was it realistic to hope for a second chance? Pushing these doubts aside, she let memories of that first camp called Hopeful nourish and encourage her. It had been held in the Entebbe Zoo, or more correctly, the Uganda Wildlife Education Center. The children had adored every moment of it, and one star appeared—Kiabo, the gift, the natural leader for future camps. The other campers had adored her, looked up to her, and learned so much from her natural enthusiasm and leadership. Kiabo, the light; Kiabo, the adviser; Kiabo, the late-night listener; Kiabo, the camp fire dancer; Kiabo, the gift.

"Sure, camp helps heal the loss of Bobby for me, but I do it for the kids, not for myself," she told herself firmly. *Self-doubt is for teens not old, I mean, mature people, like me*, she thought. But still it persisted. What had she to show for this first half century of her life? Her small apartment in Baltimore still had a huge mortgage on it. The divorce from Jeff following Bobby's death still rankled. Legal costs had cost more than she had imagined, but his words over Bobby's death still cut her. Deeply. "Careless. Stupid." These harsh nonbiodegradable words still seared her. She had heard stories of girls who were good friends with their exes. Not true for Willow Carr. Relationships since then had been sporadic. She was not a hanger-out-at-bars type. How did you meet Mr. Right? The real one—not Josh, her ex, or wanting-a-one-night-stand Jim? The answer to that question, fully documented and published, would make her first million, she told herself wryly.

Pushing aside all of these gloomy thoughts, she began packing and preparing for the ride to the airport. Washington, Amsterdam, Entebbe. A senior epidemiologist at Johns Hopkins, Willow loved her work. The longitudinal study of the HIV-positive young people in Uganda was rewarding. Medicine was improving, and most were doing well. Sure she had attended a few funerals, but overall, the trajectory was up. And camp was the icing on her work cake.

The second camp was due to start in a few days in a different location, and she looked forward to it.

Into her packing she threw a copy of her hobby. During her Uganda visits, she had read voraciously Ugandan history and stories. She told herself that she would keep trying to find a way of moving her word toward publication and even, who knows, a movie. Motion Pictures Corporation of America in LA had seemed a likely way, but all she ever received were little postcards of rejection. No contacts, no movie, she told herself. Willow smiled. This hobby was fun and had given her another perspective on Africa. Suddenly, she took the script out of her hand luggage, grabbed a pen, and wrote. This is how her creative mind often worked. Impulsive. "Alternative title, 'Love on the Nile,'" she scribbled.

After the party and such a sleepless night, Willow went into a deep sleep in the long ride to Dulles Airport. Traffic was sluggish, and she slept deeply for over an hour. Then her heartbeat and breathing quickened as she entered a period of REM (rapid eye movement) sleep. Her closed eyes darted in all directions. For most of us, this period can be peaceful, creating some lovely but confused dreams as the body prepares once more for deeper sleep. But for Willow this morning, this was not true. She saw huge tongues of flame darting around her. Each tongue had a gigantic mouth, and the mouths were screaming in unison, "Stupid! Stupid! Stupid girl!"

"We're here, ma'am. Your luggage is already on the sidewalk in a trolley."

Willow was rescued from this quite common nightmare by her arrival at the airport.

"Are you all right? Looks like you've seen a demon ghost."

Willow shook her head, recovering as quickly as she could; paid the fare with a generous tip; and replied, "I did. My ex."

Chapter

7

The smartly uniformed elevator attendant bowed and pressed the button for the eighteenth floor. Winslow Kirk closed his eyes and savored the rise floor by floor. A rise beyond his wildest dreams, certainly beyond the dice-throwing tilt at fate of his late father; a rise far beyond the shameful poverty of his early childhood; a rise to the pinnacle of power and total control. Putting aside the truth that this rise was temporary—compulsory retirement for him and dozens of other "middle-level functionaries" was imminent—and had been hastened by the swift totally unexpected vagaries of fickle fate demise of two senior staff, Winslow was determined to relish each moment. This elevation to power was where he and a few select others would, through their deliberations and decisions, control over 80 percent of the planet's gross financial product. Winslow opened his sea-blue eyes and admired his over six-foot frame, bespoke suit, and handwoven Harrod's wool tie in the elevator mirror. Despite his age of sixty-five years, he showed no paunch. He was proud of his regular gym workouts after which he rewarded himself with soothing treatments in some of the world's most exclusive spas. The door obediently and silently opened on the eighteenth floor.

"Gutenabend, Herr Kirk."

At precisely 7:00 p.m. another uniformed attendant ushered him into magnificent conference room E and then discretely withdrew. Winslow blinked, then stood for some moments on the threshold of power. Yes, this elevation had certainly been sudden. Sudden because his boss had suffered a massive heart attack while his deputy was fighting a relapse of coronavirus. Thinking of his two senior colleagues, Winslow murmured, "There but for the grace of God go I," to himself. He smiled as he realized that even his imminent mandatory retirement might now be put on hold. Taking a deep breath, he stepped into conference room E.

"Winslow Kirk, I believe? So sorry about Chip. Goodenough was a dear old chum. Vanity of vanities, eh? We never know the moment. So now you're holding the fort, what? Welcome. This is the perfect place to escape from our political masters."

Winslow took the outstretched hand of Sir Jeremy Rawlinson-Plant, the current governor of the Bank of England. Unlike Winslow, the governor had rather let himself go—slightly disheveled, body mass index off the chart, eccentric, and the late Charles Goodenough's closest mentor and confidante. He was quite brilliant. In room E, every two months, on a Sunday and always precisely at 7:00 p.m.—of course, this was Switzerland after all!—an elite group the Economic Consultative Committee of the Bank for International Settlements comprising eighteen central bank governors from the world's richest, and hence most influential, countries met in consultation. Winslow Kirk, as chairman (acting, acting) of the United States Federal Reserve System, now joined them. Winslow glanced down through the huge wall-sized windows of the circular tower block and could see the central Basle railway station. Introductions were made, and Winslow soon felt more relaxed.

During the next hour, secrets were shared, advice given, and the resulting action steps would affect the savings and investments of most of the world's people. Recently, they had tried to work in trillion dollars unison to shore up the world economy during the coronavirus outbreak. They congratulated themselves that, led by the US Fed, they had used all their capacity and technocratic competence to avert a much worse recession, even depression. A key topic this particular evening was the global Laundromat, that Washing Well of billions of dollars cleaned, ironed, folded, and spent anew. Winslow listened attentively as the discussion moved to specific money laundering situations and the ongoing Danske Bank scandal. Winslow listened carefully and then with a little trepidation asked his question.

"I wonder is it possible or practical to actually shut down a bank which has been hijacked by money launderers."

The conference room fell silent. No one seemed in a hurry to answer. The embarrassed silence continued for some time.

It was Sir Jeremy who finally spoke. "Fair question. But that would be a matter for each individual government to decide."

Winslow decided to take the bull by the horns as he replied, "Well, could we recommend such a move?"

Sir Jeremy smiled. "We could, but we wouldn't. We could discuss such issues with our political masters, but then it would be up to them to decide the next steps."

Winslow then shared his concern. "My secretary of state is concerned that Pearl of Africa Bank in Kampala, Uganda, is being used for laundering money, which may be used for terror activities."

Sir Jeremy was first to reply.

"Well, this is the first I've heard of it. The global Laundromat is mainly focused on just oligarch greed. However, the danger of transfers for terror is real. Try to find the real origin of the money being transferred and that should help answer whether it is for terror or just greed. I suggest you discuss further with the chairman of Bank of Uganda, who would then need the final go-ahead from his political masters."

The meeting over, they then repaired to a dining room overhung with two huge chandeliers that reflected on each of the place settings that were unique for each occasion. As the participants took their appointed seats, the chandelier lights were dimmed and candles lit on each of the tables. The candleholders were silver, depicting huge fig trees on which lounged several lions, their legs and tails stretching down through the branches. The fabled, truly unique tree-climbing lions of Ishasha in Queen Elizabeth National Park Uganda. The large silver holders had been created by Mavros, the creative Zimbabwean silversmith.

This was now a time of more in-depth sharing. The exquisite haute cuisine made discussion on the global economy, the fates of rich and poor, flow as smoothly as the grand cru wines, which were served in copious quantities.

Albeit temporarily, Winslow Kirk had entered heaven's portals. He wondered at his grandfather's view of heaven and muttered to him, "Grampa, I'm already there!"

"I've given my Chancellor of the Exchequer a few good lines which he uses in his idiot speeches. He's grateful, and it keeps him off my back," Sir Jeremy growled as he munched his wienerschnitzel.

"Example?" Winslow asked.

"The appearance of financial stability creates monetary value. Of course, he must replace 'the appearance of' and add 'our nation's.'" Sir Jeremy roared with laughter.

"Thanks. Must remember that for my treasury secretary. 'Our nation's financial stability creates monetary value.' Love it!"

"Thank God our political masters are only in charge of talking and not actually doing anything important. By the way, just between the two of us, I'm thinking of stepping down next year. Charlotte, my wife, is developing early onset Alzheimer's. Thought I was the forgetful one, but her situation is real serious. Some days she doesn't know who I am."

"I'm sorry, Sir Jeremy, real sorry."

Winslow placed his hand over Sir Jeremy's. The two sat in silence, each contemplating the changes and chances, the unforeseen vagaries of their own lives. Light years away from macroeconomics.

"Yourself?"

Winslow put his glass down and stared into the ever expanding jowls of Sir Jeremy. He had only ever shared his secret ambition with one other person, his mother. Would it be wise now?

"Well? Heh, I've hit a nerve, eh?"

Winslow began to reply very slowly. "I'm not married now. I feel full of energy. Retirement is being forced on a group of us. I'm going to make a bid for senator."

Sir Jeremy circled the air with his arm, indicating that his wine glass was urgently in need of a refill. Three waiters competed to oblige.

"Glamis thou art and Cawdor and shalt be king hereafter! Mad old boy, quite mad! See your doctor. Find the best psychiatrist in America. Look, I can recommend one in Harley Street. No, no, no, no. Please promise me as a dear friend you are joking. Look, you are sensible. You know how the real world works. You couldn't play Macbeth. You're too decent, too honest, too..."

He spluttered to a halt, and Winston recoiled at the harangue.

"Well, as I say, just my way of thinking at the moment. I think I would be rather good at it. I'm also beginning a new book on inequality."

"Better, much better. Do it and forget politics."

As Sir Jeremy turned to the governor of the EU Central Bank on his left, Winston stared into the central candles held by a variety of fig trees and wondrous lions stretched languorously in the branches, the famous tree-climbing lions of Uganda created in silver by Mavros, the Zimbabwean silversmith. As the candles flickered, Winslow saw in the middle of the group a young teenage girl beckoning to him. He stared. Her hair was blond, curling at the ends. In that moment, surrounded as he was with the murmur of financial voices, a mystical warmth suffused him, a peace, a happiness tingled his very nerve ends. A precious moment of glory. For this moment, this too-brief moment Winslow knew peace. The past was gone, wiped out. Maybe, just maybe, there was a future. Maybe, just maybe, forgiveness was possible. Maybe, just maybe, he could reunite the two Eleanors. His body spasmed in rapture. He smiled, then his hands shook, and he slumped forward.

Only one word came from his lips. "Eleanor?"

"Pardon me?" Sir Jeremy asked. "Look, are you okay, dear chap. You look like you've seen a ghost."

Winslow sat upright. What was happening to him? The second sight? Perhaps his mother was right after all.

"Oh, nothing, just talking to myself."

Sir Jeremy shook his head. "Have a break from it all, Winslow. Take a fresh look at your life. I mean, what do you really want? What really, really matters? Why the hell does it take us idiot men decades to finally ask that question? Sometimes it's too late. Other times, it's almost impossible to achieve what we want. I wish I had paid more attention to my wife Harriet's deteriorating condition." Sir Jeremy nodded for his large wine glass to be refilled and was now in full flow. "I mean when the chips are really down, down like a critical illness or a broken relationship or the loss of a child, what the hell does any of this really mean?" His large hand swept the room and the members of the Economic Consultative Committee of the Bank for International Settlements.

Winslow did not reply because he did not know the answer.

Some Sundays the dinner was over by 11:00 p.m., but this particular evening the diners could hear the Basle station clock chime midnight. This part of the meeting was not scripted and could take as short or as long as the participants wished. Perhaps the wines were particularly exceptional or perhaps the participants were in more loquacious mood than usual. Whichever was true, it was close on 1:00 a.m. on Monday morning before there was a general consensus that enough was enough, and at the sound of Sir Jeremy's booming voice quoting Samuel Pepys' "And so to bed," the controllers of the world's most influential central banks replied in unison, "Hear, hear!"

Winslow loved it all. He thought how much the governors would miss this unique benediction, which had become part of their routine were Sir Jeremy to step down as Bank of England governor.

Everyone felt so secure. Not only safe from any interference but for this period of time also safe from their respective governments.

The building, often referred to as the Tower of Basle, was so inviolable that even the Swiss authorities themselves required prior permission to enter this citadel. Inviolable. No security cameras were installed. Switzerland respected privacy above all else. As it transpired, this was unfortunate. No phones were permitted, and Winslow had his safely locked in his hotel suite safe. Inviolable. This made it all the more surprising to Winslow Kirk when on standing up in his place at the dining table he noticed a piece of paper sticking out from under the saucer of his coffee cup. He picked it up and read the message.

"Holy Quran Chapter (5) surat l-maidah. Exodus 21 vs 24. Abu."

Again. Abu. The brilliant user of social media to send the hate-filled messages from al-Qaeda and Islamic State. The one who was now coordinating the two. The one who this early Monday morning in the heart of Switzerland using traditional pen and paper to send a warning deep into this inviolable citadel.

Winslow pocketed the paper, walked straight up to the managing director of the tower. He had overseen the whole dinner and was now waiting respectfully for the participants to leave.

"Herr Bolanz, your office, please. Now."

Behind the closed door Winslow handed over the paper.

"Inviolable, my ass!" he told the startled director. "Fire all your staff and start again!"

Herr Bolanz's hand shook as he read the message. He walked to a large bookcase and pulled down a Bible and looked up the Exodus reference. After all, this was the Switzerland of John Calvin.

"I don't know the Quran, Herr Kirk, but Exodus says, 'An eye for an eye, a tooth for a tooth.' Looks like a warning message. Please leave this with me and the Swiss authorities. I assure you we will investigate thoroughly."

Winslow was not convinced; and as he sat in the room, he took Herr Bolanz's iPhone, took a photo of the message, and sent it immediately to his secretary of state.

Back in his hotel suite, Winslow undressed quickly and collapsed onto the large king-size bed.

Winslow pulled out the small pocket Bible his grandfather had given him fifty-five years ago and looked more carefully at the Exodus quotation. He had come across it only last week while hunting for a golf glove. The sand grain in the oyster itching again? In order to protect itself from irritation, the oyster quickly covers the uninvited visitor with layers of nacre, also known as mother of pearl. Was Winslow's new mystic sense growing more beautiful?

"An eye for an eye, a tooth for a tooth."

Abu had one purpose. Revenge for a personal slight. But what?

Winslow read further. It referred to harming a woman who is subsequently hurt or dies. The punishment was to follow exactly the harm caused. "If any harm follows, then you shall give life for life, eye for eye, tooth for tooth, hand for hand, foot for foot, burn for burn, wound for wound, stripe for stripe."

"Life for life." Winslow shuddered. But what had all this to do with him? He wasn't even a politician, thank God. He immediately checked his iPhone.

"Nothing back from Jeannie yet," he murmured to the goodnight chocolate on his pillow. *What the hell's happening in our crazy world*, he wondered.

But there was a message from his mother's iPhone number in Connecticut. He dialed quickly.

"Lost? Wandered off? Aren't you supposed to be her carer, her minder, for God's sake?"

Winslow stood by the bed a little unsteady from his recent libations.

"Are you Judy?"

"No, sir, she's now off. I'm Hadley. We changed shift, and somehow in between she...Sir, should I call the police?"

Winslow sat down heavily on the king-sized bed. In the past few weeks his mother had been disoriented, confused, and yet at times totally lucid, especially in matters relating to his granddaughter Eleanor. Before this Basle trip, she had sat with him as she once more went over events nearly fifteen years ago.

"We should have taken her in when your daughter and her husband died at sea! She was three for God's sake, so lost."

Winslow stared out into the dark Swiss night. Dark as his regrets. Yes, this might have happened had not fickle fate so cruelly intervened.

Then her final words before he left. "You've all I've got, Win."

"Sir, are you still there? What…?

Winslow started from his reverie. "Hadley. Fix it. Find her!" he told the latest low-wage recruit at Constant Care as he pressed the little red icon.

*****

Winslow lay staring at the ceiling. Tree-climbing lions and a young blonde teen danced in his brain.

It's real, he thought.

How often had his mother assured him that she was convinced that he had it? It, the second sight. He heard her voice.

"You're a Kirk, lad. A Kirk. You are not a seventh son, but you were born on July 7. Seven, seven, you see. He is likely your ancestor. Believe me, you have it, lad. You have it."

He opened Robert Kirk's seventeenth century writings *The Secret Commonwealth of Elves, Fauns and Fairies* and began reading in the middle.

> In 1676, when there was some scarcity of grain, a marvellousillapse and vision strongly struck the imagination of two women in one night, living at a good distance from one another, about a treasure hid in a hill called sithbhruaich, or fairy hill. The appearance of a treasure was first represented to the fancy, and then an audible voice named the place where it was to their awakening senses. Whereupon both rose, and meeting accidentally

at the place, discovered their design; and jointly digging found a vessel as large as a Scottish peck, full of small pieces of good money, of ancient coin; which halving betwixt them they sold in dishfuls for dishfuls of meal to the country people. Very many of undoubted credit saw and had of the coin to this day. But whether it was a good or bad angel, one of the subterranean people, or the restless soul of him who hid it that discovered it, and to what end it was done, I leave to the examination of others.

"The second sight—I have it," he told himself. "I'm a Kirk."

Winslow suddenly thought of the note in the Tower of Basle. He jumped up and closed the book as he called his secretary of state.

"Jeannie? You never replied."

In her Adams Morgan apartment, the secretary of state was luxuriating in a very hot bath and, like Sir Jeremy and Winslow, was contemplating the vagaries of fate in her own private life.

"Hello, Buttsy, nice to hear from you. Still slumming it in Basle, are we? A message? No, I've not seen that yet. I do try to have some sort of life beyond State, you know. Wait, I'm reading it now."

Despite the seriousness of the message he had received, Winslow smiled as he heard his name, Buttsy.

"I'll share it with our geeks, but I don't expect much progress there. Seems we are always one step behind. Meet me as soon as you arrive back. The drone strike on Abu? Honestly, I don't know. Our Somali contacts have disappeared. And if he is instructing his people to send messages like this to you in the heart of Switzerland, then it confirms we missed him. It clearly refers to an ancient blood feud, which would stop major conflict between tribes. One person's death can be atoned for by the death of another in the opposing tribe. In Somalia, as in other parts of the world, clan loyalty is supreme, followed by family followed by religion. Looks like the clan or family loyalty has been broken, and our drone strike broke it."

Winslow put the phone down. In the wee hours of the Swiss night, all ambition seemed to desert him. For the umpteenth time, he relived the erratic wind change on Long Island Sound. The gybe. The whiplash of the boom as it scraped his head.

"Martha Jane," he muttered to one of his myriad hotel pillows. Why did absurdly expensive hotels need so many pillows? After all he only had one head. He made a note to mention this in his new inequality tome. "Martha Jane, I'm sorry. What do I do now?"

Like the crashing waves that followed the yacht's gybe, loneliness swept over him, a chasm, an emptiness, which he felt sure could never be filled engulfed him. He tried to take comfort in his numbers that he loved. The mystery of the change that was taking place since the days of Maynard Keynes. Keynes stated almost as an axiom that 66 percent or two-thirds of the world's wealth was always shared back to the labor that produced it. This had been true for decades until a few years ago when this percent had shrunk to 59 percent and was shrinking further following the coronavirus outbreak. Hence, inequality; hence, unemployment; hence, anger; hence, chaos; hence, terror. He had spent months contemplating this mystery. Then recently his mother had reminded him that the world's richest company Apple was now valued at close to $1trillion. Only a dozen of all the world's countries had a gross national product more than that. What would Keynes have made of all this?

As the Basle railway station came to life in the early morning, the chairman of the Federal Reserve (acting, acting) fell into a fitful sleep.

Chapter

8

The crisp British English voice was almost cheerful.

"The number you have dialed is not available at the present..."

"Shit," Winslow Kirk muttered to the flight departure board in Amsterdam's Schiphol Airport departure area. Calls to Uganda were not possible at this time. His Bank for International Settlements meeting over, he was now returning home.

Basle. Amsterdam. New York. He glanced up at his KLM flight to New York. "Delayed."

"Shit, shit, shit," he repeated. Numbers men often have limited vocabulary. He glanced at his phone's world weather app. New York was blanketed in snow. A true nor'easter was pummeling the whole East Coast from Maine to the city that never sleeps, which might now have permission to sleep a little once more after its coronavirus slumber.

Then the flight information changed again. "Cancelled," it said.

Winslow turned and decided to regroup in the luxury Crown Lounge reserved for business-class and first-class passengers. As he turned, he saw a woman laughing at him. He stared, annoyed. She tossed her red hair as her tea-green eyes met his.

He walked up to her and stopped. "What's so funny?" he asked.

She was certainly not dressed for a New York blizzard. Winslow stared at her green cotton slacks, very tight fitting, and light-yellow T-shirt. Her smile was disarming.

"Oh, I'm sorry, sir," she said. "Wasn't laughing at you. I was just watching a YouTube video on my phone. It's hilarious. Flight delayed?"

Winslow nodded. "Worse. Canceled."

"Oh, too bad. Mine is delayed several hours. Something about clearing vultures from Uganda's Entebbe runway. They were munching on a couple of goats killed by a service vehicle."

Winslow wasn't used to such casual, light banter. He shrugged and started to head toward the safety of Crown Lounge.

"Have you ever done bungee jumping?" the woman asked.

She might well have asked had he had played a round of golf on Mars.

Winslow replied, "Of course not. Why the hell would I do that!"

"Look at this." She showed him the video as it restarted.

A young girl leapt from a makeshift and rather vulnerable-looking wooden platform clutching in her arms a pink teddy bear. She screamed as she plunged headfirst toward a fast-flowing river. In her outstretched arms, the teddy bear's head, now with a ridiculous unicorn hat firmly glued to it, plunged into the river. The unicorn skimmed the waves. Then together they sprung back into the air, sky clear and blue above and beyond them.

"A young woman I assist. She's called Kiabo. She sent it on her new friend's phone, a volunteer. She calls it 'Eleanor and pink teddy discover source of river Nile in Uganda,'"

Eleanor. Teddy. Suddenly this fellow stranded traveler had the chairman (acting, acting) of the Federal Reserve's undivided attention.

"Let me see the teddy's ears."

"Ears? Why?"

Winston studied the video and stopped it as teddy's face was closest before the dive. The teenager's curly blond hair swept over her face, which was still wreathed in mischievous freckles.

"Right ear missing. Was eaten by our dog, Rex the King. This is my granddaughter, Eleanor."

In that moment, in the airport departure lounge, the chairman of the Federal Reserve's life changed. Again. A plethora of emotions swept over him. A life of measured carefulness was over. In that moment Scrooge had awakened on Christmas morning. In that moment his heart sang and took control of the rest of his being. He handed the phone back. He didn't think you could take prayers back again, but he now wondered if he could cope with this sudden answer to his "Lord, surprise me" prayer. His voice shook as he stuttered the next words.

"Where did you say this was taken?"

"Uganda."

Just then a very frazzled fellow traveler staring at the canceled notices on the board pushed by with her three young children in tow. "Ugandabekiddin' me," she muttered.

Willow glowered at her.

"When was this taken? Is she still there? How can I see her?"

Even as he asked the question Winslow sensed a breath of the numinous, a spot of grace.

"Yesterday. Yes. Come to Uganda. We can call her when we arrive."

The answers were that simple. Winslow held the astonished woman in his arms and pulled her toward him. Their noses brushed, and then he kissed her. A few fellow stranded passengers smiled. This wasn't exactly the clock at Grand Central Station, New York, but hey, it would do.

Without another word he strode toward the KLM ticketing office, leaving a very bewildered woman standing under the departures board. A platinum credit card and Crown Lounge membership made the transaction simple. Visa? Fifty dollars cash payable at destination. Clothes? Banana Republic set delivered at a 20 percent premium directly to the lounge.

With money all things are possible, Winslow told himself, then wondered for a brief moment if this quote was slightly wrong. From the deep recesses of memory, he heard his grandfather preach on Christmas Eve the words of the Angel Gabriel to Mary, "For with God nothing will be impossible." That mischievous grain of sand was turning in the moneyman's soul.

In the Crown Lounge, he ordered a large pot of coffee. His mind raced. Eleanor. Could he face seeing her again? How best to apologize for abandoning her all these years ago? Would she forgive him? Remorse, regret, even fear. His body shook. A few tears plopped into his coffee cup. His iPhone dinged.

"Hadley! What's going on?"

"It's Amy, sir. And we found Mrs. Kirk. It was early this morning."

"How is she? What happened?"

"Sir, she was down at the beach looking over Long Island Sound paddling in the sea, snow billowing around her. It's freezing now, you know."

"And?"

"Sir, she was calling out to the ocean. Some poetry, I think. So beautiful, I wrote it down. 'Things fall apart; the center cannot hold; Mere anarchy is loosed upon the world.' Then she started screaming, 'Eleanor, Eleanor, Eleanor!'"

"That's her poet Yates again. Amy, let me talk to her now."

"She is sedated."

"Now, I said now!"

"Yes, sir."

"Mother, it's Winslow. I think I understand your paddling in the freezing Sound. I too am confused. Listen carefully, Mother. I have found your great-granddaughter. She is in Africa, and I promise I will bring her back to spend some time with you."

"Africa, Win, Africa?"

"Yes, I am flying there now. Please relax, and don't worry. What you and I want more than anything else in the world is going to happen, I promise."

Then he heard his mother's deep breathing.

Winslow put down his coffee cup and looked over the lounge, mainly businessmen and a few very well-dressed women. He caught the eye of one woman, who smiled sympathetically at his tears. He nodded. Would Eleanor forgive him, even accept him at all?

"Final boarding for your flight to Rwanda, sir." The Crown Lounge manager tapped him on the shoulder.

"Rwanda? I am going to Uganda."

She smiled. "First stop is Kigali, Rwanda. Forty minutes. And then KLM will whisk you on to Entebbe."

*****

Winslow sank into the business class seat. It was spacious but rather old fashioned in that it did not become a full bed as on more regular routes. Still the seat beside him was vacant, and he desperately needed time to reflect.

Then his phone rang.

The stewardess, who was pouring champagne at the time, shook her head. "One minute, sir, then switch off as we prepare for takeoff."

The voice on the other end seemed to come from Pluto.

"Chairman. Sorry I've kept missing your call. How can I help?" Caleb Karuhanga's voice spoke volumes of his bewilderment and at the same time how pleasantly surprised he was to hear from the new Fed Chief.

"Thank goodness, I got you. I am on my way to Uganda. Now on KLM. I'll explain when I get there."

"Wonderful. I'll arrange a driver and hotel. No worries. Look forward to welcoming—"

The line cut.

Winslow smiled as he had a sudden flashback to his last post-cardiac session with Doris.

"And remember. Not too much excitement. Take things easy. We are just starting the process of mending this heart of yours. You only have one heart, you know. Remember Dr. Ostreicher pointed this out to you just before surgery. He said it helped him since he couldn't operate on the wrong one!"

If only Doris could see me now, he mused.

His reverie was interrupted by the stewardess.

"Quickly, ma'am. We are about to takeoff. This is your seat."

Winslow looked up.

Her cheeks were flushed scarlet. Her tea-green eyes held his gaze. Her Celtic-red hair tumbled over her face in unison with her rushed demeanor. She plopped down in the seat and fastened her seat belt. The stewardess swiftly handed her a glass of Dom Perignon champagne. The bubbles tickled her nose.

"So this is how the 1 percent live?" she muttered. "Or is it the .01 percent?" She held her hand over to Winslow. "Willow Carr. The girl you keep kissing. Mix-up. Two of us back there near the toilets in steerage had the same seat number. I gave up my seat, and well, here I am in a brave new world. Quite a coincidence, isn't it?"

Coincidence.

Winslow smiled and, astonishing himself, found himself mimicking his grandfather, but only in his thoughts. *Willow, if you think this is a coincidence I wish you a very dull life.*

She sipped her champagne. Her left hand brushed her hair aside to reveal a pretty suntanned face. Winslow now had time to admire her bonny features.

"Could get used to this, you know," she muttered. "Do you one percent people know that half the world's population have the same wealth as the top richest three people?"

Winslow tried to hide his embarrassment. "Well, yes, I had read that. Inequality is growing, and it's tough to stop it."

Willow's response startled him.

"Bullshit. It's simple. Haven't you read *Finance in the 21ˢᵗ Century* by the Frenchman Thomas Pickety? Solution is called taxation. Tax the rich till they squeal and then redistribute."

"Oh." Winslow appeared not to have thought of this solution.

"Even the great Warren Buffet accepts that a 35 percent tax on highest earners is reasonable, but your political master just won't do it."

Acerbic tongue. Acerbic mind.

Yet that grain of sand in the oyster turned and twisted and scratched and irritated, all the time pearl making.

Winslow's disappointment at having his peace disturbed was somewhat alleviated by his intrigue as to who this woman was and, of course, a lead to his granddaughter. Her most striking feature was surely her hair. Red. Not dyed in punk fashion. Real. And like her legs stretching out into the seat in front, long. Wine was served before dinner. Not small little bottles you might buy in steerage but good wine from bottles poured into the glass in front of you. A limitless supply.

"Cheers, Chairman!" Willow said as she raised her glass.

Winslow recoiled as if stung by a bee.

"So we meet again, Mr. Kirk. I knew I recognized that face. Chair of Fed Reserve, isn't it?"

"You know me?"

"Come on, Mr. Kirk. I read newspapers, and I follow you on Twitter."

Willow was clearly enjoying this new world.

"And you got the job because of death and sex!"

Winslow glowered at her. *So rude. Who the hell does she think she is? And she didn't even pay to be up here in my world.*

"Look, when we arrive, you need to call your friend and let me speak to my granddaughter."

"I spoke to Dorcas Isiku, one of the camp leaders. She gave me Eleanor's iPhone number. Kiabo and Eleanor have already arrived at Camp Hopeful on the banks of Lake Albert."

"Camp Hopeful?"

"It's a camp a local nonprofit has started running for HIV-positive young people. An experiment. Many of the kids are my patients."

"You're a doctor?"

"I'm an epidemiologist with Johns Hopkins, and I am doing a longitudinal study of young people who have been receiving therapy treatment for AIDS over a fifteen-to twenty-year period. As part of the study, we help pay the cost of a Kids Camp for HIV positive children, and I will be attending that."

Winslow admired her enthusiasm and obvious love for the young people.

"You do realize there is a travel advisory?"

Willow's nose twitched. "Who cares! If it's safe enough for the chairman of the Federal Reserve, it's safe enough for me."

Winslow shrugged. "How are the Ugandan children doing then?"

"Some have died for a variety of reasons. Poor nutrition is one. They need a decent diet to be able to tolerate the medicine. And then some just stop taking the medicine because of stigma from school friends. A lot of reasons. But on the whole, success rate is high. They are truly great kids. One or two are now graduating from university. So you decided on a quick search for Eleanor, eh? An impromptu journey to the Pearl?"

"Pearl?"

"You know Winston Churchill called Uganda the Pearl of Africa. He loved it, visited by rail and steamer in 1908. He said, 'The kingdom of Uganda is a fairy tale. You climb up a railway instead of a beanstalk and at the end there is a wonderful new world.'"

Winslow nodded. "I am also going to visit a bank called Pearl. Pearl of Africa Bank. Now I see how it got its name."

Willow was not convinced. "A baby bank! Don't believe you. You only deal in billion dollar entities."

Winslow was not used to being contradicted. He scowled. "Well, also the terror situation."

Willow thought for a bit. "Kiabo was caught up in the Entebbe bombing. I want to hear her story. I hope your granddaughter is okay. Abu, the leader of al-Shabaab, has been behind so much chaos in East Africa. But you know what I really think?"

Winslow shrugged. *Here's another economics lesson from this charity worker.*

"Our real war is our war on greed. Our greed is the heart of inequality."

"Title," Winslow said quickly.

"Pardon me?"

"Thank you. You've just given me the title of my next book on inequality. 'War on Greed.' You do keep up with current events, don't you?"

"Mmm. I met him, you know. Abu."

Winslow thought he had misheard. "Excuse me?"

"I met him."

Winslow wasn't sure if she was winding him up. "How?" he asked simply.

Willow grinned. "You big boys, the well-upholstered fat cats, think you know everything. You would do well to listen to the simple foot soldiers like me who frequent the less salubrious parts of the globe. During the idiot, ill-conceived Bush/Blair invasion of Iraq, I was seconded to a Red Cross team, which visited Abu Ghraib prison in Baghdad. I spent a few hours in the prison. A couple of prisoners were brought out. Abu had traveled from Somalia and was leading the insurgency around Baghdad. He was the only one who spoke. And you know what he told me?"

Winslow shook his head. For some strange reason his education was just beginning, entering kindergarten.

"In English, he thanked me very much for this admission to what he called Jihad University."

Winslow nodded. "He's not wrong. Whole pockets of Islamic State oozed out of Abu Ghraib after the massive prison break."

Willow held his gaze. "Your drone strike got him, didn't it?"

Instead of saying, "Classified," Winslow said, "No, Willow, it seems we missed Abu. We think he is in East Africa now. In fact I received a strange message purportedly from him."

"What did it say?"

"It was just a verse from Quran, also Exodus. 'An eye for an eye, a tooth for a tooth.'"

"Revenge?"

Winslow shrugged.

"Shit."

"My sentiment exactly."

The two traveling companions began to laugh.

"You know what my Scottish grandfather used to say?"

"Nope, never met him."

"Laddie ye maun laugh for ye daurna' greet."

"Translation, please."

"My boy, you must laugh for you dare not start weeping."

Willow was quiet for a few moments and then said, "Winslow, may I call you Winslow? The problem with Abu is more complex than we think. I believe he is bipolar with catastrophic mood swings. Whether he's on medicines now, I have no idea."

"How the hell do you know that?"

"Why would he let it be known that he has a data base of top terror folks? It's not logical. Also just think of all the trauma he's gone through. His recent decision to enter Kenya and maybe Uganda is senseless."

Winslow shrugged. "Dunno. I guess we're all kind of complex in our own way."

*****

For the next few hours both read and listened to some music. The wine flowed and soon Willow's papers dropped to her lap and her head rolled over onto Winslow's shoulder. He froze. A few strands of her hair tickled his nose, and he gently pushed them away. There was something so simple, so natural about her. He relaxed and allowed her head to nuzzle into him. His nose twitched. Lavender with a touch of green apple. Her ear piece was still emitting a song. He recognized James Taylor's voice. The words floated out. "Angry Blues."

> I can't help it if I don't feel so good.
> Gonna sit back here and watch this cloud roll by.

It was as if she was telling him all about herself without saying a word.

The stewardess came by, smiled at this cozy scene, and refilled the glasses.

Winslow watched her lips moving in her dreaming.

Willow's brain was working in her dream as the music and the wine prompted thoughts.

I'm up in cloud nine. Isn't that supposed to be a buconic tranquil paradise No, it's what mother warned me, the highest of the cloud types, cumulonimbus, with the most complex and dynamic inner life, hence is the most dangerous of all cloud systems.

Winslow's own thoughts then strayed to his grandfather. On a summer excursion they would swim together on the West Sands of St. Andrews with the cathedral and castle above them. He taught him how important breath was for life. And then shared what he had learned as chaplain in the Royal Navy during World War II, how to hold your breath for a long period underwater.

His hands were by his side. His feet were together. Six feet under water, he swam using what the Navy SEALs now call the fifty-meter two-minute challenge. Slowly, he released his breath, creating bubbles of oxygen that raced for the surface. One minute passed. Two minutes. The record for a polar bear is just over three minutes, his grandfather told him. But for humans, two minutes was near the maximum. He gasped and sucked air. A crazy flashback.

A manuscript was still on her lap, and he picked it up.

"Journey to the Heart, an original screenplay by Willow Carr."

A coincidence? *How many surprises can I take*, he asked the bottom of his wine glass. This was the manuscript sent to his mother in the hope of an angel funding for a movie. No wonder she knew who he was. He opened it at random and read.

*****

EXT. BRITISH CONSUL JOHN PETHERICK'S HOUSE – CONTINUOUS
The house has the British lion and unicorn crest on the front door. Petherick has gone south with his new wife, Kate, to rescue Speke and Grant on their journey back from source of the Nile in Uganda. However, many suspect he is doing ivory trade. The house has been left to them by Petherick.

EXT. INSIDE OF BRITISH CONSUL'S HOUSE. UPSTAIRS BEDROOM, ON VERANDAH BED IS COVERED IN MOSQUITO NETTING – AFTERNOON.
Florence and Sam look down on garden where several animals roam about. Giraffe, waterbuck, a camel, baby cheetah, and several monkeys. One baby monkey swings onto verandah and jumps onto Florence's shoulders from a tamarind tree.

FLORENZ
Eee. Get off, Wallady! Get off!"
SAMUEL BAKER
(laughs)
You've named him already. He's yours now.
The monkey jumps onto a tamarind tree branch watching them intently.
A servant brings gasses and drinks onto the verandah and places them on a table near the bed.
FLORENZ
Sukran Khalil. You may go now. And no one is to disturb us.
KHALIL
Sukransiit.

He bows and leaves them closing the bedroom door. Sam and Florence drink in silence. The sun is now setting and temperature dropping slightly.

FLORENZ

I've never felt so hot in my whole life. Africa is like living in a permanent oven. In Viddin we had wonderful snow in winter. What I'd give to have some now.

Florence removes her dress.

SAMUEL BAKER

Ceylon was hot but nothing like this. But we'll get used to it. The human body can adjust so well.

Florence folds back the netting slips onto the bed. As she does so, she waves Sam's handkerchief, which she had picked up at the Cairo dance.

FLORENZ

I believe this is yours. I think it's time for your to claim this back, Mr. Baker.

Sam looks a little flustered, stares over the balcony at the animals. A giraffe has its head almost up to the verandah. The monkey, Wallaby, screams encouragingly. Sam undresses and slips under the net onto the bed. He gently strokes Florence's hair.

SAMUEL BAKER

Never?

FLORENZ

No, never. There is a first time for everything.

EXT. CONTINUOUS

Wallady screams, the giraffe moves closer, then we hear Florence's gentle moan.

FLORENZ

Don't stop, Sam, ever, ever, ever.

My heart is yours to the very heart of Africa.

*****

Winslow's mind was reeling.

Suddenly Willow shuddered and pulled away. "Sorry! Excuse me! I'm not used to all this free booze." She sat up straight and moved well over to the far side of her large seat.

Winslow grinned. "No problem. For a moment there, I didn't feel so lonely. Perhaps I'm not a shoulder to weep on but at least one to lie on. By the way, I glanced at your manuscript. You sent it to my mother. I advised her not to be a soft touch."

"Yes, that's how I recognized you. Son of a top retired publisher."

"Not as chair of the Fed?"

They both laughed.

"My hobby. I love the research. The screenplay is based on a true life story. But getting it to a movie is another leap."

The two were silent for some time as the plane sped over Egypt, Sudan, and Congo.

Then Willow suddenly asked, "Do you ever wish you could undo something in your life?"

Winslow's reply was dreamlike. "A breath of air, a change of wind."

"For me it was a match. Just one match."

"Clouds rolling by can be real dark."

"True."

Without revealing much of themselves, there was an understanding that each of them wished to "undo" some past history in their lives. Neither appeared to be in any hurry to reveal what that was.

Willow dozed again, and Winslow dropped a pure white handkerchief, neatly ironed at the Gnomes Hotel Basle, into her carry-on bag. The moneyman's African odyssey had begun.

Part 2

Chapter

9

"Zika? Isn't that the virus causing so much heartache in Brazil? I mean babies born severely deformed when their mothers are infected?"

Winslow's arrival into Africa was at least so far smooth. Entebbe airport arrivals had been okay, swift, in fact, as Mr. Caleb Karuhanga's driver, JB, whisked him through the VIP section loudly, exclaiming to all who would listen that this gentleman was VVVIP.

"Chairman of the Federal Reserve in America, don't you know? For him cash dollars are just like grains of rice to you people."

Embarrassing but somehow effective. But then things slowed down.

"My friend here, Ms. Carr, will travel with us. Not to Serena Hotel but to..." Winslow glanced at Willow.

"Speke Hotel," she said. "Called after nineteenth-century explorer who documented the source of the Nile."

JB glanced at this far-from-corporate visitor. Technically, this was his day off, but for drivers in Africa, there was really no such thing. He had been drinking local Bell beer in a sports bar, Just Kicking, and watching his soccer team Manchester United's hero M4 play for Uganda against South Africa for World Cup qualification when the call came from the Central Bank governor.

After a quick wash and change of clothes, plus a few peppermints to neutralize the booze fumes, he quickly arrived at the government garage where the almost-new Mercedes Benz car rested. He then received the second call.

"Oh and, JB, no delays, you, hear me. No shopping for cheaper *matoke* on the way. Straight to Serena. And tell the Chairman that I plan to be with him at 7:00 p.m. this evening."

Now he was in a dilemma.

"Sah, my boss didn't say anything about another visitor," JB objected.

"Don't worry I'll explain to him later this evening. Let's go, please."

So they set off for Kampala, but after a few miles, Willow said, "Please, can we turn left here. I need to see Kiabo's grandmother. She lives just on the edge of Zika Forest."

This was when Winslow asked about Zika.

Willow smiled. "Yes. The virus was discovered by a British scientist in a monkey here in the 1940s. He called it after the forest. The virus has subsequently spread to humans."

"Chief, my boss, he said no delays." JB was wondering how his beloved Ugandan team was faring and if he could make it back to see the second half.

"Look, Kiabo is your granddaughter, Eleanor's friend. I promised her I would look in on her grannie. She hasn't been so well since the bombing. We are so close to her here. Please. And we have JB here to translate."

Winslow shrugged.

"Well, I'm not meeting the governor till later this evening. We have time. Let's go, driver."

JB's scowl spoke volumes. His already low opinion of women now went below ground zero. He reluctantly turned left toward Zika Forest. His mood deepened as he was instructed to stop at a small bakery so that Willow could buy six large loaves of bread for Granny and her family.

Winslow had now changed into his Banana Republic kit and felt more comfortable. He wondered whimsically if he was now entering the wonderful new world that his father's namesake Winston had spoken of all these years ago.

With directions from Willow, JB carefully parked the Benz on a dirt track above Granny's home. He held his nose as two piglets scurried away. While the others walked toward the simple two-room shack, JB shooed away a couple of curious kids and then stood guard over his source of livelihood.

As they approached the ramshackle two-room shack with very rusty metal *mabati* roofing sheets, Winslow saw an elderly and stooped woman come toward them.

"Jajja," Willow said. "I've arrived. Winslow, please meet Granny Maud."

The woman knelt down and greeted the visitors in her native Luganda. Winslow looked into her bright eyes. Her dress was threadbare. She wore no shoes. Her two remaining front teeth welcomed them with a grin.

"JB! No one is going to steal your Benz. Please come down and translate," Willow yelled. "And bring the bread!"

JB's scowl deepened darker. Did she not understand that he was the personal driver of the top bank boss in the country? Snail-paced, slouched, he joined the group.

Granny led them into her little home.

As Winslow turned into the house, he bumped his thigh on a wooden handle. "What the...!"

Willow laughed. "Be careful, that's Grannie's leasing business." She took his hand as he stooped under the small door.

"What leasing business?"

"I bought it for her. She leases this wheelbarrow out for about fifty cents a day," Willow explained.

"Who wants it?"

"It's a decent business, you know. Folks need to move sand or cement or bricks or even patients to the clinic. She told me she once had a three-day lease to a man whose wife had died. He needed to bring food and drink to his house for the wake. Then he used it to help those who had drunk too much to get home."

Maud gave Winslow the seat of honor, a plastic chair whose fourth leg was rather wobbly. The others sat on a long school bench while Maud took her place on the mud floor. Two chickens shrieked as JB practiced a soccer shot on them, anticipating Uganda's winning goal against South Africa. They flew out into the dusty yard. Winslow glanced at a poster stuck on the wall behind Maud. It showed a variety of hairstyles with the title "Last Chance Salon."

"Maud here has been looking after not just Kiabo but many other grandchildren. Her two daughters both died of AIDS, and she was left to bring them up."

Winslow tried to steady his chair by adjusting his weight in the opposite direction of the wobbly leg.

"Please tell her how much I admire all she has done," he said.

JB faithfully translated and then Maud's reply.

"I even have some savings, but now my account in Pearl of Africa Bank is no more. I went there yesterday, and it is closed. I suppose my money is gone."

"How much did she have?" Winslow asked.

There was a spirited discussion among JB, Maud, and Willow. JB clarified the situation for Winslow.

"This bank had a big problem. Some big people used it to launder some of their stolen cash. Then another group may have used it to move money to buy arms for al-Shabaab in Somalia. Yesterday my boss shut it down."

"Shut down?" Winslow repeated incredulously. "Shut down?" His work had already been done for him.

Winslow wanted to sit back in relief but was still worried about the safety of his chair. Precisely what his secretary of state had wished for had happened. But was it, as usual, too little and far too late?

"How much did Maud have in her account?"

Willow grinned. "She says it was a fortune—28,750 Ugandan shillings."

JB who was lightning fast with all aspects of finance said, "Seven dollars and seventy-seven cents at yesterday's exchange rate of 3,700 to a dollar before her bank was shut down. It's a big problem for her."

Willow was hugely enjoying this dialogue between the chairman of the Federal Reserve and one of the world's poorest women.

"Don't worry, Jajja. The Chairman here will take this matter up at his next Bank for International Settlements meeting in Basle," she said.

Winslow stared at Maud's serious face and smiled. Yes, the chairman of the Federal Reserve was beginning to enjoy this fresh perspective on world finance. The 777 numbers sounded familiar. Only last week the *Wall Street Journal* had announced that in the past three months worldwide financial deals had clocked a record $777 billion. Suddenly his mind flashed back to chapter 3 of his financial tome titled *What Is Money For?* On a whim, he said to JB, "Please ask Granny what is money for?"

Granny stared in bewilderment at this rich visitor who knew so little about the world of finance. Without a word, she put her hand on her thin stomach.

"For food, Winslow, for food!" Willow said with a grin.

Another lesson in finance, Winslow thought.

"Don't worry about your cash, Maud. It will be secured. I promise you," he assured her.

Winslow handed two twenty dollar bills to Maud, stood up, and turned to go. But Maud held Willow's hand and pulled her back into her home.

"Ibrahim?" she said.

They all went back inside and sat down again.

"Who is Ibrahim?" Winslow asked.

Willow put her head between her hands. "He is Kiabo's brother, same mother different father but same jajja, grandmother.

And he is with Kiabo now at Camp Hopeful for recuperation and, well, just for her comfort."

"What happened?"

"Long story but he was with the Ugandan Army in Somalia, you know part of the peacekeeping army we Americans fund, our boots on the ground, and he was captured. Tortured too. And then in the moment of the drone strike, he escaped and is now home again. In a bad way. Really bad way."

To Granny, Willow said, "He is with Kiabo now and will visit you soon, Jajja."

What happened next surprised them all. Granny started waving her arms around and walking up and down in a frantic rage. All the time she was yelling in her local Luganda.

"What?" Willow asked.

JB translated. "She seems to be mad as hell at God," he said.

"Be more specific, JB," Willow insisted.

"Well, she said, 'You are Ibrahim's God. You are my Christian God. You are the Jews' God. So why are we all fighting over you?'"

Willow spoke first. "She is so right. Ibrahim. Abraham. He is the founding father of all our monotheistic religions. Poor Ibrahim. Why did he have to suffer so much in Somalia?"

Everyone was silent for some time, contemplating the mystery of suffering.

Then Winslow muttered, "I've always seen myself as an atheist ever since my dad's death."

"You know what it means?" Willow asked. Then without waiting for an answer, she went on, "From the Greek *athos* refers to 'lonely ones, those whom the gods have abandoned.'"

"I guess that's how Granny feels today."

"Yes," Willow agreed and took Winslow's hand as they returned to JB's Mercedes, the source of his income.

As Willow was dropped off at her Speke Hotel, they agreed to meet the next morning. As she exited the car, he saw, to his surprise, two large pots full of red and pink begonia.

"Lovely," he murmured. "Red and pink, you know."

"Pardon?" Willow's flushed face matching her bright-red hair pushed back through the open window.

"Nothing. Just admiring the flowers."

"Not another coincidence, I hope?" Willow asked.

"Coincidence? Don't believe in it," Winslow muttered.

"Coincidences. Not for moneymen!" Willow shouted as JB gratefully slammed his Benz door.

*****

"Chairman, this is a surprise. First time in Africa? Can't believe our little economies can be of much interest to the US Federal Reserve or Bank for International Settlement."

Caleb Karuhanga sank into a deep armchair on the spacious verandah of Serena Hotel. Night-scented jasmine mingled with the smoke from Caleb's Romeo and Juliet cigar.

Thank God I agreed to stay on as governor and delay retirement a bit longer, he thought.

A waiter brought his drink.

"What's that?" Winslow asked.

"Juice of six limes with two dollops of wild Ugandan baobab honey, crushed fresh ginger, and two bottles of tonic water with lots of ice."

"May I?" Winslow asked. "Very nice. I'll have the same."

"Well, even if I haven't made it to your Tower of Basle, at least the mountain has come to Muhammad. Sorry, is that a bad analogy in these troubled times?"

Winslow smiled as he surveyed the rich foliage and fountains in the hotel gardens.

"But, Winslow, may I call you Winslow? I believe you are also here to see your granddaughter."

Winslow Kirk squirmed in his seat. "JB?"

Caleb laughed. "Having a driver in Africa is like having a therapist but also a spy."

"Your driver, JB, said you have already shut down Pearl of Africa Bank?"

"JB, he knows more about the country's economy than I do. Yes, I did. I never thought that the plague of the global Laundromat would come to Kampala. I mean, we are hardly Danske Bank, Deutsche Bank, HSBC, or RBS, are we?"

"My concern is more the money transfers directly to al-Shabaab to foment terror all over East Africa and beyond."

Caleb Karuhanga dropped some ash into the huge green tanzanite ashtray. "War on terror? My president thinks it is. I'm not so sure. More likely war on greed. Greed dot com is the problem."

Willow's words and now the title of his incipient tome, *War on Greed*. "How come?"

The governor of the Bank of Uganda stared into the black African night. "Coltan, old boy, coltan. Our iPhones, gaming consoles, iPads, etc. and our whole social media just can't get enough of it. And it's all next door in DR Congo. The Saudi Arabia of coltan! We need to look at the source of the funds."

"That's exactly what Sir Jeremy—you know, England's bank governor—said. Find the source."

"Six months ago the largest of the coltan mines, about a hundred kilometers over the border from Lake Albert, was commandeered by some mysterious group. Illegally commandeered. They then ironically used a team of genocidaires, you know the gangs who were instrumental in the Rwandan genocide and who now hang out in DR Congo, to guard the mine. Today, these boys are just thugs for hire. The mine continued to thrive and then began transferring all revenue through Pearl of Africa Bank. From there to God knows where. I think Kerala in India was part of the route. I brought it to the attention of our president and then a couple of days ago shut it down. He still thinks it's the source of our recent terror. There were certainly large cash exits, but after that we have no idea how it was used. Personally, I don't buy it. It's just greed." Caleb was silent for some time and then continued. "Unless…"

"Unless what?"

"Well, unless al-Shabaab had started pressurizing the new mine owners and skimmed off what they needed in return for a guarantee of safety in the environs of the mine in Congo. Eastern Congo has no government and is ruled by whoever steps up and pays up."

"Incredible. If what you say is true, then the terror tentacles can reach across borders."

"Terror without Borders," Caleb said. "Islamic State was created out of the crazy invasion of Iraq, and now the same terror boys are heading here to East Africa after you Western countries couldn't agree on Syria and took out the Kurds."

Winslow replied slowly. "I agree. We were wrong to leave northeast Syria in such bad shape with Turkey going after the Kurds, who were doing such a good job imprisoning thousands of ISIS until now..." His voice trailed off.

The two bank governors sat in companionable silence for some time, then Caleb continued his train of thought.

"Quis custodies custodiet?"

"I beg your pardon? Luganda?"

"Latin, old boy, Latin. My Latin master at King's College Budo outside Kampala, one of Africa's oldest schools, which our king of the Buganda, the Kabaka, attended and many of our top politicians. Our royal school."

"My grandpa went to a royal school too. Royal High School of Edinburgh."

"That was my Latin master's old school. He was always boasting about it. He was a crazy Scot and loved Latin more than anything else."

"So what does it mean?"

"It's a proverb. 'Who guards the guards?' Maybe the answer to that will lead us to the real source of the laundering."

Just then Winslow's phone dinged. A message from Willow.

"Kiabo has sent another message through your granddaughter's phone. Here is the number. Sure, she'd like to hear from you."

Winslow's heart stopped. His hand shook. "Would you excuse me, please," he muttered.

He wandered into the luscious greenery. Caleb smiled. Winslow did not call immediately. For the first time in the last few years, he was now afraid. Fear. Will she talk? Will she be at all happy to be contacted? Could he be forgiven? Tentatively, he tapped the numbers.

"Hi!" A young lightsome optimistic voice.

"Eleanor. Listen, this is Winslow Kirk, your grandfather."

Silence on the line. But thousands of cicadas filled the African night with their laughter, complaints, chaos.

"Eleanor. Listen, things are not at all safe. There is a travel advisory. Let me arrange to take you back home."

"Grandpa? Really?"

"Sure, it's me. I saw the YouTube video of you and pink teddy. How is he?"

"Fine. Camp Hopeful is wonderful, you know. I am here with Kiabo. She met me when I arrived. It was after the terrible bombing, and she took me with Daddy's Amex card to see the tree-climbing lions in Ishasha, then bungee jumping at the source of the river Nile at Jinja."

"Look things are not so good, Eleanor. Please come down to Kampala, and we'll head home together."

Again, a deafening silence, then a single word. "No."

The line cut.

Winslow slumped back to his chair on the veranda.

"Kids, eh?" Emmanuel said. "No rhyme nor reason to them."

"She doesn't want to be rescued."

"Well, neither did David Livingston when Stanley showed up to take him home."

"What should I do now?"

"Well, as I said, the mountain must go to Muhammad, you know. Go to Camp Hopeful."

"How?"

"Leave that to me." Caleb sat back and stared into the night sky.

Orion's belt was at its most prominent. He recalled that the three stars of the belt were actually light-years apart, but we at distance see them in perspective.

Perspective, yes, that is what we need now, he thought. Then he began talking as if to himself. "If you think talking to kids is hard, try talking to my president right now. Everyone keeps well away. He is like a mountain gorilla with toothache."

"Are deposits in Pearl of Africa Bank secure?"

"Grannie?"

Winston nodded.

"JB told me about the fortune she has amassed there. The value of two Perrier waters in your local Starbucks."

The two men laughed. A waiter brought refills.

Then Winston asked, "How true is it that Abu could actually be in the country?"

"Very possible. We are trying to ascertain any safe havens he may use. But across the border in Congo (DRC), every hut and cave and forest can be a hiding place."

"Yes. I called her and asked her to come down here right away, but she refused. She is volunteering at a children's camp for HIV-positive children near Lake Albert. Camp Hopeful, it's called. I'm worried about her. You see, I received a threatening note about revenge from Abu. I'm now wondering if it concerned Eleanor."

"We can't understand why he would risk coming so close into East Africa. Yes, you would be wise to ship her out soon."

"I spoke to her and asked her to come down to Kampala, and we can head back home together."

"And she said no?"

"You have grandkids?"

Caleb laughed. "Don't ask me how many! But yes, they are a different species. What happened to our traditional values of respect and obedience?"

The two central bank chairs sat in silence, each pondering the mystery of youth.

"Tell you what though," Caleb said. "Tomorrow evening our top soccer player who is here to play for Uganda in a World Cup qualifier will be whisked up to the camp by chopper. Seems he is a donor and, according to JB, has fallen for one of the camp counselors. You could hitch a lift and maybe persuade your granddaughter to leave."

"Sounds a good idea. Face-to-face should persuade her."

"Suppose you would like your girlfriend to go as well?"

Winslow spluttered. "Look, I, girlfriend? What do you mean?"

Caleb roared with laughter, and then the two men yelled in unison, "JB!"

"She was planning to go by road, but this would be wonderful."

"Look, I'll arrange the flight for you both."

"Thank you, sir, I would appreciate the help. I'll also call our ambassador and secretary of state tonight to inform them of my whereabouts. Might be mighty surprised."

Kaleb laughed. "Politics, it's nuts. Look, just get Eleanor out safely and leave poor old Uganda to the Central Bank governor."

The two men sat in silence as the stars Orion's Belt in perfect perspective in the African night sky wheeled their way west.

Then Caleb started murmuring to the night sky, "Simul ipsa precatur Oceanumque patrem rerum Nymphasque sorores *centum* quae silvas, *centum* quae flumina servant." He started to laugh. "Since I quit the demon drink, my mind has become incredibly clear. You've reminded me of my old Latin master. McCallam, he was called. McCallam, same as a Scotch. I used to drink it till, well...we had to memorize huge chunks of Virgil. Just in case you haven't already translated it, here goes. 'Together she entreated father Ocean and the sister—Nymphs who guard a hundred forests and a hundred streams.'"

"Centum." Winslow nodded. "Centum."

*****

Back in his lovely hotel suite, Winslow found sleep impossible. So many thoughts flashed through his brain. Baobab tree honey.

Eleanor? All young people think they are immortal, and she clearly felt no more danger despite having arrived soon after the Entebbe bombing. Willow. Acerbic mind like his mother. A hundred forests and a hundred streams. He shook his head and felt into his carry-on luggage. What else had his mother packed from the attic? He pulled out some dog-eared papers. "Greed, the Greatest Sin of All," his grandfather's last sermon in Duddingston Edinburgh before retirement. Winslow relaxed into a chair, looking over the hotel gardens.

Our text this morning is from the Gospel of Luke chapter 12 verse 15. The words of the Lord Jesus. "Beware of greed!" Our Lord tells us to beware of many things but this is the most important. The old fashioned word for greed is *covetousness*. The Greek word *pleonexia* which Luke uses means "an inordinate desire for riches." A desire that smothers all else. A desire that smothers the life of the greedy one but also smothers the lives of the poor. The iron law of greed is "more is better." The loving way of God touches us with generous and happy hearts. Dear friends, I beg you this morning, be rich, be rich, be rich, but towards God alone. Relish the riches of his forgiveness, the wonders of his grace.

Winston could feel again the stone walls, the wooden pews of Duddingston Kirk. He smiled as he imagined his grandfather in full flow. He crawled into bed and fell into the deepest sleep he had known for some years. All thought of informing the ambassador and Jeannie Backhouse was forgotten in dreamless slumber. Tomorrow is, as they say, another day.

Chapter

10

Dr. Obed Ochola wanted camp fire to start right away so everyone could sleep early and be refreshed for the next day. But like many of our best-laid schemes, this wise plan was soon interrupted. Out of the black African night, a light appeared and shone brighter as it came slowly down toward Camp Hopeful. The children all spoke at once.

"It's a spaceship!"

"People from Mars have arrived!"

"What language do they speak?"

The children drew closer together, and a few began to cry. The green-colored chopper had large marking on the side.

"Uganda People's Defense Force," it announced.

The doors opened, and three people jumped out, ducking under the still rotating blades. Then three soldiers leapt out after them and moved swiftly to the back of the campers. When the visitors were safely in camp, the soldiers jumped back into the chopper. The doors closed, and the Bell 412 helicopter rose up into the night sky.

Dr. Obed walked over to greet the three latest campers.

"Oh, it's you, Auntie Willow," he said. "Welcome, welcome. Please welcome Ms. Willow Carr back to camp. You know all this was her idea in the first place. We started camp one just last year."

The children yelled their happy welcomes.

"Auntie Willow," Kiabo yelled. "Welcome, welcome!"

"And this is Eleanor's grandfather, Winslow Kirk," Willow said.

The two men shook hands.

"Please welcome our new visitor to camp."

"It's Eleanor's grandpa," Kiabo yelled. "And pink teddy's! Eleanor, come on, say hello to Grandpa!"

The campfire sizzled. A few logs settled more comfortably into the embers. Sparks flew into the dark sky behind the retreating chopper. Eleanor and Winslow stared at each other, the few feet between them a real-life distance of fifteen years. Fifteen lost years. The campers remained eerily quiet as if sensing the tension. Winslow was now sure that this had all been a huge mistake. Just like signing off on the adoption, showing up here was another mistake. His bright-blue eyes asked a thousand tentative questions. Why had Willow brought him here? Why had he been persuaded by Caleb Karuhanga to make this trip to camp?

It was Eleanor who blinked first.

"Grandpa? You came to see me?" she almost whispered.

Winslow, now convinced that enough words had been spoken, strode toward his granddaughter, arms wide open. Eleanor ran into his embrace, still clutching their only link, pink teddy, still with the missing ear. The camp broke into cheers and ululations.

"Eleanor, I-I-I'm..."

"You came," she whispered. "I always knew you would. I mean, I hoped you would, so I could tell you I will never forgive you. Never!"

Winslow stepped back. He had been right all along. This trip was crazy. Eleanor now had her own life, and he was not to be part of it. He was glad of the camp bustle around them all camouflaging both himself and all his emotions. He was pleased that the tears coursing down his cheeks were hidden by the dark and campfire smoke. Eleanor moved off and sat by Kiabo. Mosquitoes hummed around. Lake flies swarmed up from Lake Albert to any light they could see.

The children needed no introduction to the third visitor. They screamed their welcome to Uganda's most famous son.

"Our man, M4, M4!"

Tall, muscular, fast, and at just under six feet and only twenty-two years of age, here was the complete athlete. Uganda's most famous soccer player had just returned to play for the national team in a qualifying game for the forthcoming World Cup. Mac Kiwanuka had scored the winner against South Africa, which edged them even closer to World Cup qualification for the very first time. But his day job was as Manchester United's brilliant striker in England. He had achieved the aspiration of every African schoolboy and was now rich beyond anyone's wildest dreams.

"M4! M4!"

They couldn't believe he had come to Camp Hopeful. The visitor waved and wandered nonchalantly to the campfire. Magnificent Mac the Marvel from Mbarara (M4) now rivaled even President Yoweri Museveni's title of M7. Dr. Obed scowled a Queen Victoria "we are not amused" scowl. M4 strode over to Dorcas Isiku, the senior camp counselor, and kissed her.

"I promised Teacher Dorcas I would come, and well, here I am," he yelled.

When the excitement had died down, M4 sat down by the fire. Tomorrow he would lead a soccer clinic with everyone followed by a match in which he would star. Dr. Obed then turned to Winslow. He saw a *bon viveur* who had not arrived from Mars but from Connecticut. In a flash of insight, he saw a luxury lifestyle but at the same time was impressed by the man's fit frame.

"Thank you all for coming. Many of you already know Teacher Dorcas Isiku, who even taught some of you here at Sir Samuel Baker School. She is now working with the Ugandan Army, helping them to catch tyrants." He then turned to M4. "You are a busy man, and thank you for your two great goals against South Africa. World Cup here we come!"

The children yelled, ululated, and cheered.

"But more than that, he has generously agreed with some advance earnings to match the grant by Eleanor's late mother to a new children's wing at Christ the Healer Hospital."

More cheers and some kisses were thrown in M4's direction.

"He will also donate to Kids First Foundation, so some more school fees will be available."

This added promise had not yet been discussed with the footballer, but M4 did not seem to notice. Dr. Obed was always alert to all fund-raising opportunities.

Again there was uproar from the young people.

"Campers, our campfire songs and discussion will be delayed ten minutes while our new guests get themselves settled in."

M4 was shown to his room that Dr. Obed pointed out was a single room. Teacher Dorcas and Eleanor were in charge of the girls' dormitory; and he, Dr. Obed, the boys.

*****

Willow threw a few more logs onto the campfire. After some time Obed wandered over and sat beside her.

"You don't like him, do you?" she said.

"What? Who?"

"Oh, come on, Doctor. I wasn't born yesterday, you know. The heart also needs healing."

The doctor shifted in his folding camp chair.

"Maybe you can help, Willow," he said.

She said nothing.

"Dorcas was a brilliant English teacher, and we were in love, and I thought moving, you know, toward marriage. But then her nephew was abducted to Congo and became a child soldier there. She stopped teaching and led a group to find him. She succeeded in bringing him home but never went back to teaching again. Instead, she joined the Ugandan Army and is now in military intelligence. She's changed, Willow. She seems much harsher now. I think we've grown apart."

Willow burst into another uncontrollable fit of giggles.

"It's not funny!" the doctor said.

"Sorry, I've become like a teenager in these past days. On my journey, I met Winslow. My granny once said something to me, and the truth of it is only now dawning for me."

"What?"

"She said, 'People aren't always what they seem.' And then she winked at me and continued, 'Especially men.'"

"Well, thanks very much! It's Dorca's changing that we're talking about, not me."

"No, not you, silly. I meant the soccer hero. He loves the kudos, the adulation, and Dorcas used all her female wiles to bring him here for the kids camp, but it doesn't mean she's in love with him."

"Really?" The doctor seemed amazed and gratified at this. "Well, if you have a chance to speak to Dorcas, please let me know which way her heart is turning."

"Okay," Willow said. "But my own heart is not exactly stable either."

The doctor continued, "She's more beautiful than ever now. When she was a teacher, she was a lot fatter, but now she's slimmed down in the army. Lots of exercise. Her skin is now smooth and perfect. Problem is, it makes her more attractive to many more men, you see."

"Oh, Doctor. Faint heart ne'er won fair lady. Don't you be giving up."

As if on cue, Dorcas, along with Eleanor and Winslow, came out of the darkness and joined them.

"That was quite an entrance we made," Willow said. Then turning to Dorcas, she said, "Dr. Obed tells me you work with military intelligence."

Dorcas flopped down on an empty camp chair.

"Yes, quite a change from teaching, but I'm seeing a different world, and it's improved my running times."

Dr. Obed nodded. "You know that *Dorcas* means a 'gazelle.' She is Uganda's fastest woman, and I'm sure will be part of the national team when the Olympics come along. Marathon."

"I've heard that Dr. Obed loves fast women," Willow said with a mischievous grin.

As Willow, Winslow, and Eleanor joined the young people round the campfire, Willow looked back to see Dr. Obed and Dorcas in deep discussion.

*****

The campfire began with songs and dancing. As the moon rose above the lake, the mood became more reflective. Annabella shared with the group all that was happening to her at school as friends noticed she was taking medicine. She wept as she told them how these so-called friends had deserted her when they learned that she had AIDS. But the star of the evening was Kiabo.

"Start at the beginning and tell us what really happened at the Entebbe Tarzan Inn," Dr. Obed asked. The inn was called after Tarzan since the very first *Tarzan* movies had been shot there, around the Botanical Gardens. He hoped that this would help dear Kiabo to come to terms with what had happened in the terror attack.

Eleanor told her story, embellishing what she had related to Teacher Dorcas some time before. As Winslow listened, he told himself he should never have come. A crazy whim and a mistake. And knowing the deep secrets from the secretary of state, he now realized what danger Eleanor and, indeed, all of them were in.

Kiabo stood up and moved away from smoke billowing from the fire. Then she faced her friends. Near the back of the group sat Ibrahim, her brother, same mother different father. He was eating well but spoke only to Kiabo and even then very little. He had been given fresh clothes, but his wounds were deep, both skin and soul. He watched everyone very carefully from deep inside his own skin. He held in his hand a small pouch, which he would never release to anyone. As Kiabo moved forward to speak, she noticed that her brother was writing something on the ground. The number 100. Then as he had done so often before, he started rocking and murmuring nonsensical words, "Kanya ma kan."

Kiabo put her hand on his head. "Brother, I have told my story. One day you may tell yours."

Ibrahim's head shook violently. "Never ever," it said silently.

Kiabo hugged Eleanor and sat down. The camp was silent. This beautifully told tale had touched each of them. Dr. Ochola led them in prayers with special mention of Alano and Albert and then suggested that it was time for sleep.

Winslow had never known such total calm in a large crowd of people. As he watched the evening star, Venus, set in the west, he found himself wondering about his own life. Was a senator bid even possible? Was it what he wanted? Did he want to spend the rest of his life alone?

As the group moved off to the dormitories, Winslow stayed by the fire, still thinking. Dorcas ambled over and joined him.

As if speaking to himself, Winslow muttered, "I'm so lonely now."

Dorcas's eyes stayed fire fixed. "I think it's the biggest disease of the first world," she observed. "Much shopping, many instant communication tablets, but a deep chasm of emptiness."

Winslow nodded but said nothing.

"Do you know what Nicole Kidman said some days after receiving her Oscar?" Dorcas continued.

Winslow shook his head.

"She said, 'I was holding a gold statue, and I was the loneliest I've even been.'"

Winslow smiled. "Well, I don't have a gold statue, but there are times when I stop and think and then I'm lonesome."

"Truth is, Winslow, I'm also lonely," Dorcas continued.

"But you have such a busy job, Dorcas, and colleagues in the army," Winslow said.

Dorcas was quiet for some time, then spoke slowly. "I don't know who to trust anymore, sir. The boys who come back from

Somalia peacekeeping are often quite changed, and I wonder if the Muslim ones have been influenced by some al-Shabaab agents. I actually knew one of the boys who planted the bomb."

"Isn't that just post-traumatic stress?"

"No, I mean, something more. I wonder if some have been converted to radical Islam."

It was wonderful for Dorcas to have someone to speak to, and Winslow seemed such a warm, understanding person.

She continued, "I watch everyone, especially those who have returned from peacekeeping in Somalia. I have become a very suspicious person."

"Your job is not easy, that's for sure," Winslow observed. "By the way, I need to ask you about a strange number written in the sand here by Ibrahim—100. One hundred. You see our secretary of state spoke to me about a terror plan involving Centum, one hundred."

Dorcas scratched her head. "Kiabo showed me it. Ibrahim wrote it, but I've no idea what it means. I feel at times I know so little. That's what leads to the loneliness, you see. I'm ever suspicious. Wasn't it T. S. Eliot who wrote of the loneliness of a suspicious person?"

"Perhaps," Winslow said. "I know numbers more than literature. Maybe you need to find someone to share all this with, someone who cares about you." Winslow looked in the direction of the boys' dormitory.

Dorcas shrugged. "A doctor maybe? Do you do match-making on the side, Chairman, when you're not busily searching for a long-lost granddaughter?" she said with a grin.

Chapter

11

As a wonderful reprieve from all that had happened to her, Kiabo was now relishing each moment of camp life. She was vivacious, exuberant, loving each morsel of succulent plenteous food, embracing new friends, enjoying freedom from nasty jibes, and a brief reprieve from a life of grinding poverty with Granny. Kiabo was certainly an unlikely companion for Eleanor, the adopted daughter of Tag Borner, the Hollywood movie mogul. In striking contrast, Eleanor was sometimes unappreciative, moody, and at times downright rude. Yet instead of repelling each other, these two teenage girls were in a short time drawn together and developed an extraordinary rapport. As an escape after the horrific Entebbe bombing and with help from Eleanor's platinum card linked to her father's, they had spent a few idyllic days visiting the renowned tree-climbing lions in Ishasha deep in Queen Elizabeth National Park, then done bungee jumping at the source of the river Nile in Jinja. Now they were together in Camp Hopeful, which Eleanor's mother had funded before her sudden death. Eleanor volunteered and help post blogs to the simple website that had been set up for the camp.

The setting of this second Camp Hopeful was lovely. As a result of temporary cessation of oil drilling and persuasion from Dr. Obed Ochola that corporate social responsibility was in order, the accommodation at Robben Oil Exploration camp was copious, and with a few imported cooks, the food was excellent. The location was just below Baker's Fort as the plains drifted down toward the Rift Valley, with the Nile stretching languorously out of Lake Albert, then north to Sudan and Egypt. A few Ugandan cob dotted the arid plains, so well camouflaged they seemed invisible. Forty teenage boys and girls, all of whom were HIV-positive, had come together for a week of friendship, learning, fun, and adventure. They came from all over Uganda. This was now the second time that Dr. Ochola's new nonprofit Kids First had put together such a camp. The children spoke a tower of Babel mix of languages—English, Luganda, Lugbara, Acholi. But it was the personal sharing that was so incredibly real. Well, most of it. Eleanor was still quite reticent about sharing some of her pet hates in camp. Food was very carbohydrate, but all others campers adored it. Mosquito bites were actually sore. Eleanor was sending out daily blogs, and Dr. Obed was using it on his nonprofit website.

> My new friend Kiabo told me on our morning pre-breakfast walk to the Fort that she had borrowed her pair of very old sneakers from a friend."
>
> "Borrowed?" I asked her. "What do you mean?"
>
> "They have to be given back as soon as camp is over," she replied. "We were told we needed to bring sneakers to camp or would not be admitted."
>
> Then the youngest of all the children, Rose, shared her story with the group. She began with a question. "What does disclosure mean?"
>
> Kiabo explained to her. "As you know, in order to be allowed to come to camp, we had to be told our HIV status. Usually, it's your mother or another very close relative who will tell you—that's disclosure.
>
> Rose nodded. "Well, my mother took me aside and told me she was not my mother but my aunt. My mother died when I was a baby. Then

she told me I had HIV/AIDS and would now be allowed to go to camp."

What I can't understand is how Rose is reacting so reasonable with it all. She is so serene and happy and really enjoys each moment with us all.

As Eleanor finished her blog and sent it off on her iPhone, a group of the girls gathered round her and Kiabo. The boys were off at some distance, involved in a very serious soccer match between Manchester United and Arsenal with M4 as the main attraction. Among the girls was a very tall gangly girl, Robina. She called out. "Tell us again about your magic closet at home, Eleanor. Show us again how it works."

Eleanor smiled. She opened her iPhone and showed them a few photos of her closet door with computer panel in front and then some of her clothes emerging.

"Well, it's simple really. You see you type into the computer panel the type of clothes you will need. For example, for a night club with a certain theme and perhaps colors you prefer. Then the closet will deliver a selection of clothes for you to select."

Kiabo shook her head. "But how do the clothes get into the cupboard, and how does it know so much?"

Eleanor laughed. "Once every so often clothes companies come to the house and replenish and even add new lines of clothing."

"Is it free?" little Rose asked.

Eleanor shook her head. "Quite the opposite. I think it costs a fortune, but my father pays," she said.

In this dialogue, Camp Hopeful had brought together one of the world's richest and some of the world's poorest girls.

The group of girls squealed with delight at this amazing discovery.

"But look at my designer T-shirt!" Robina said. "From the Gap!"

The group stared at her now very faded and slightly frayed shirt.

"My uncle is a porter in Owino Market in Kampala, and he is very friendly with a fat lady who sells clothes. You know, imported from America and Europe. We call them dead white man's clothing."

"What did this one cost?" Diana asked.

Robina rolled her eyes and winked mischievously.

"Who said anything about paying? Uncle Caleb said she was a close friend, I mean, very close! He tells her she has the biggest bottom in the market, and she adores him. So you see, this shirt was a result of such flattery."

Kiabo decided to change the subject and asked Eleanor again about her father.

"Imagine having a father who is so important. I mean making movies, wow! You must be so proud?"

Eleanor glared at her. Then she stared straight down the Rift Valley.

"I hate him!" she muttered.

Kiabo recoiled as if struck by a puff adder. "Eh!" she yelled. "No, no, you cannot say that! You must show respect. Why do you say such a wicked thing?"

Eleanor then shared her deepest secret. "My mommy, the one who adopted me, died when a car hit her head on. It was driven by a young man who had his dog on the passenger seat. The dog saw something out of the driver's window and jumped over the young man. *Bang*. She never had a chance."

"Sorry, please," Kiabo murmured.

"Oh, but it's worse, much worse. I came home from school early...I wasn't feeling too good. Maybe I knew just knew something was wrong...Anyway, I came home and found Daddy with a strange woman. She was still there when the police arrived with news of Mom's death. Since then, he is so busy, busy making movies and money, I hardly get a chance to see him."

"But now you have your dear grandfather."

"Hah! He abandoned me. I will never forgive him for that!"

Another group of girls joined them and demanded to see the pictures of the magic closet that delivered clothes on demand. One girl called Maggie made her request.

"Let's say I have a date with, you know, our man M4 Uganda's top footballer…"

Her friends laughed at such an improbability. "He asked me along because he is meeting with the president and he will be wearing dinner jacket with black tie. What will magic closet give me?"

Eleanor was happy to join in the fun. "Well, let's see, I would type into the computer screen black-tie function and my preference, say for a short black dress with silver shoes, maybe a couple of pairs so I can choose."

Maggie was still not satisfied. "But how does it know your size?" she asked. As she spoke, she touched Eleanor's blond hair. "So soft," she said. "Does the magic closet do shampoo as well? Did you bring the cupboard to camp?"

Everyone laughed and cheered. Eleanor threw back her head and laughed, a real honest-to- goodness laugh. Not a supercilious put-down sneer but a joy-filled laugh.

Funny thing, happiness, she thought. *It's breaking into me in the heart of Africa.*

*****

That evening, as the African sun was giving up her heat before the campfire started, Kiabo and Eleanor wandered off. They walked in silence for some time. Suddenly the silence was broken by the flap, flap, flap of the wings of the three-crested crane birds. The girls watched as they circled the valley and then gracefully landed one by one beside the Nile.

"Beautiful," Eleanor said.

"I'd love to fly like them," Kiabo said. "You can jump into an airplane, but I never could."

"Maybe I can arrange something," Eleanor mumbled. "We'll see. As you know, I have my father's credit card with my name on it, so such things are possible."

Kiabo was not convinced. "You know, it's just not fair that all of the campers are so poor and you, Eleanor, like a princess, have everything," she said suddenly.

Eleanor looked very uncomfortable.

"I guess life isn't fair," she observed. Then wishing to divert from such an uncomfortable subject she asked, "Tell me, what is your earliest memory?"

Kiabo scratched her head. "Anger," she said. "Anger."

"What do you mean?"

"I was carrying water from a well in a clay pot. An older girl pushed me. I fell, and the pot broke and spilled the water."

"Where's the anger?"

"When I got home, my grandmother screamed at me, 'Poor, we are poor! We cannot afford to break our precious pots!' What about you? Your earliest memory?"

Eleanor thought for some time. "It's a smell memory. A chorine-and-bleach smell from a swimming pool."

"What's that?"

"Well, it's a pond made in your garden where you can swim. I have one in the garden and another in the house so we can swim in winter time."

Kiabo tried to imagine such a thing in her grandmother's little two-room hut that she shared with four other children but shook her head at the impossible image.

"I jumped into the garden swimming pool, but was so young, I couldn't swim. My father jumped in and pulled me out. I remember the smell of chlorine and my mother screaming at my father, 'You were supposed to be watching her!' They sometimes screamed like that, but then they both died."

"You see," Kiabo said triumphantly. "Yours was smell memory but also feeling memory. Your parents were angry like my grandmother."

The girls stopped walking as two vervet monkeys chased each other.

Behind them a man stepped out into the dusk and lit a local Sportsman cigarette. Kiabo stared. Returning to camp, they passed the kitchen area and the same man appeared. He looked up. Kiabo dropped her gaze and quickly went past him. After a few moments, she said to Eleanor, "It's him."

"What are you talking about?" Eleanor asked.

"I'm sure. It's the man who left the bomb at Tarzan Inn. I saw his face in the light of a cell phone. Small and brown. Somali, I think."

"We better tell Teacher Dorcas," Eleanor said. "Let's keep an eye on him."

Eleanor shuddered as she recalled Kiabo's description of the bombing. Nothing in her young life came close to such an experience. All her concerns about being cool, being accepted, being in rather than out just paled in comparison. The two friends made their way back to camp.

"Teacher Dorcas!" Kiabo yelled. "Come. I think I saw him. The man at Tarzan Gardens!"

Dorcas went back with the girls to the kitchen area and searched. Questions to the staff revealed that no such worker was part of them.

"I'll send a report right away to Mbuya Barracks in Kampala," Dorcas said.

"If you see him again, let me know, but don't let him know you recognize him." If true, this was a worrying development.

*****

Back in camp Kiabo and Dorcas kept on talking as girls do.

"You know this morning Rose asked me what disclosure was. She's such a sweet innocent kid. She told me her auntie told her she was not her mother. Her mother died when she was a baby, and she was looked after by the aunt. She was then told she had AIDS, and since she had been disclosed, she could go to camp."

"I love Rose. She also asked me what a virgin was. 'Are you one?' she asked."

Eleanor laughed. "Well, are you?"

Kiabo had no chance to reply. Two of the boys rushed down the hill and called that campfire was starting. They dragged the girls back to camp.

The campfire began with songs and dancing. As the moon rose above the valley, the mood became more reflective. After evening prayers, Dr. Obed dismissed the children. Willow, Eleanor, Dr. Obed, Dorcas, and M4 sat round the campfire.

To Dr. Obed's critical gaze, M4 was seated rather near Dorcas. Willow pulled over a camp chair and pushed between them.

Instead of heading to the dormitories, Kiabo and Eleanor walked up to Baker's Fort, which was now a ruin. The explorer had used nearby stone and anthill sand for cement. He had used it to keep his ammunition safe and dry. Several large borassus palm trees sounded it. A little sign read, "Fatiko 1872-1888." Eleanor admired the wide expanse of Africa's Rift Valley, a million miles of marvelous Africa in one sweep of the eyes. The plain was dotted with hundreds of flat-topped acacia trees, excellent perches for migrating birds.

She turned to Kiabo. "Well, are you?"

"What?"

"Come on, what we were discussing. A virgin."

Kiabo tried to hide her embarrassment by adjusting her "score" hairstyle.

"You first," she said.

"All right. Well, it's been touch and go at times, and boys can be very persistent. But yes, yes, I am."

Kiabo continued to play with her hair.

"I am and I amn't."

"That's ridiculous. Either you are or you're not. I mean, you can't be a little bit pregnant, only pregnant or not."

Kiabo had never ever been challenged like this before. This American girl was so—what was the expression she had heard her use—"in your face."

She spoke very slowly so softly that Eleanor had to move closer to hear her.

"I haven't had sex with a boy, but I was infected with HIV/AIDS."

Eleanor now wished she had never brought up this topic.

"Look, Kiabo, it's okay. We can leave it there."

"No, you asked. My mother died of AIDS, but I was not infected by her. When I was fifteen, I visited my auntie Bella up north here on a Lake Albert island. One night a gang of the Interahamwe boys, the genocide people from Rwanda, attacked us, stole canoes. And I was gang raped by them. That's when my infection began."

Eleanor began to cry. She hugged her friend as tightly as she could.

"I can't imagine. I'm so sorry, Kiabo."

"But now I'm trying to forgiven them. I am grateful for what I have here now."

"I never would. Never."

"Your poor grandfather has come looking for you. You need to welcome him."

The two girls stood in silence, hugging each other. The Rift Valley descended into a dark and a deep understanding silence. The two new friends knew that words would pollute this perfect sound of silence. A special friendship began that evening.

Chapter

12

Winslow stared, enthralled. On the lakeshore, Eleanor and Kiabo, now inseparable, shrieked and laughed. Bright equatorial African sunlight sparkled off the waters and illuminated Eleanor's blond curls. In a flash, Winslow saw Benson's painting, "Eleanor." He had been so right to purchase it. It did indeed depict his granddaughter. He wondered if at that moment his mother was admiring the painting in their home. His heart leapt at the thought of his being able to reunite them soon. This would now be a time of happy contentment for Eleanor's great-grandmother. But first she needed to accept him. Maybe not forgive but at least accept. So engrossed was he that he did not see Willow arrive until she sat beside him.

"Hot, eh! Not a breath, not even from the lake."

Winslow had left her finishing off an inspection session of the HIV medicines each young person was taking. Emphasis was put on the importance of regular drug intake and a balanced diet. This was more complicated as many of the campers told her the truth about their home situations and the paucity of cash and therefore regular decent meals. She then did in-depth interviews with some of the campers.

"A breath? You were going to tell me about the breath of wind that changed your life."

Winslow smiled. "And you were to share your match story. You first."

Winslow watched her face redden and thought how lovely she looked.

"Go on. Two people wanting to redo their horror moments. But they can't, can they?"

Willow stared into the distant horizon. A heat haze had settled over the lake. Then slowly at first but then faster and faster she told her tale.

"My son, Robert, Bobby, who was three was in our vacation trailer with me. He was playing with matches. I grabbed them from him, told him how dangerous they were, and put them in my pocket. I received a call on my mobile and went outside for better network. A minute, no, maybe two or three minutes passed. As I finished the call and turned toward the trailer, it exploded and burst into flames. I froze, then ran toward it, but the flames were fierce. I dialed 911. I...I...I...well, Bobby died."

Winslow put his arm around her. A fish eagle left its perch in a nearby tree and swooped down to the lake to catch lunch. After a few moments of silence Willow, went on.

"Gas had leaked from the cylinder, and Bobby might have still had a match in his hand. I don't know. I lost him, and sometime later, I divorced. That's it, the match story. That's all. Well, almost all."

"Almost?"

"'But still keep something to yoursel' Ye scarcely tell to ony.'"

The moneyman's eyes looked heavenward.

Willow laughed at his ignorance.

"Robert Burns's 'Epistle to a Young Friend.' Good advice by the way."

Winslow told her his own tale of the boating accident and Eleanor's subsequent adoption.

"Well, at least you have one person to hold on to, little or now not-so-little Eleanor. I have no one."

Winslow said nothing of her recent rejection by Eleanor.

As Willow spoke, one of the campers little Rose called her over to ask her advice. She got up and without another word marched back to camp.

Winston's whimsical mood continued, and he opened up Willow's manuscript, *Journey to the Heart*.

*****

SPEKE

(lays out maps)

The Nile flows from Lake Victoria to here in Gondokoro but in between it also flows into another large lake. The Munyoro people call it Luta Nziga, the dead locust lake. It is another important source of the Nile, and the armchair geographers at home will criticize me for not finding out more about it. It may also be near the so-called Mountains of the Moon, which could discharge waters into it. I will be criticized for not investigating it further unless…unless…

SAMUEL BAKER

(claps his hands)

I, that is, we, Florence and I, will go and confirm this second source of the world's greatest river. It will be an honor. Florence and I are prepared to undertake the journey. Also

(diffidently)

The resultant fame may help our entry into Victoria's England.

SPEKE

Go, Baker, and I wish you God speed.

He begins to write details and maps in Baker's journal

SPEKE (CONT'D)

Grant and I will speak well of your rescue when we return. But by Jove where is that Petherick? He was commissioned to assist me here.

SAMUEL BAKER

Nowhere. There is talk of him running ivory to supplement his consul ivory.

SPEKE

Despicable, what? Also, I suggest that we take your chereamie Florence back to England so that you can move south alone.

SAMUEL BAKER

Out of the question, old boy. She has never been to England and will need my introductions. Apart from which I need her for the journey south. She is lion-hearted, not a screamer like some women.

******

As he finished reading, Willow rejoined him.

"Well, can it be a movie?" she asked.

"'Not a screamer like some women,' Dunno. It's kind of mirroring our journey to the lake. Eleanor tells me the man who adopted her is a movie mogul, so you better ask her."

"Good idea. Wow, what a contact. By the way, I saw poor Ibrahim again. I think I know what he keeps muttering."

"Tell me."

"*Kanya ma kan.* It's how all Arabian fairy tales begin. It means 'It was or it wasn't.' You see, the myth is yours to believe in or to deny. *Kanya ma kan.* Once upon a time."

"Days like this I would love to know more than just numbers. You surprise me. But what the hell does it mean. He's just delusional."

"Maybe, Winslow, maybe. But on the other hand, maybe not."

Putting the manuscript back in his briefcase, Winston then strolled with Willow over to Camp Hopeful. The camp was drawing to a close. Lunch of the final day was over, and preparations were ongoing for departure early the next morning.

*****

Winslow saw Dr. Obed sitting in the shade of a borassus palm tree. M4 had already flown back by helicopter to Kampala. The doctor sat alone, wondering about the long-term effect of camp on the young people. Had his experiment been useful? He seemed to be murmuring to himself.

"Lord, bless each of these wonderful youngsters and all who have visited and helped us." He looked over to where Ibrahim was slouched against the kitchen room wall, unmoving. "And bless dear Ibrahim who has suffered too much. And help me to understand your holy word given to St. Paul when he was so sick. Second Corinthians 12:9, 'My grace is sufficient for you. For my strength is made perfect in weakness.' How, Lord? Please explain."

Winslow walked over to him and sat down.

"So almost over?" he murmured.

"I loved the way the young ones mimed to the music of their local pop stars with such great names—Chameleon, Julianna, Bobi Wine," he said.

Dr. Obed smiled but did not reply.

Winslow continued, "This has been a special time, Doctor, for me. Thank you for introducing me to my long-lost granddaughter Eleanor. Unfortunately, she doesn't seem so enamored of me. No forgiveness for poor Grandpa. But still this trip has already changed me. I feel younger already!"

Dr. Obed laughed. "When we were at the Royal College of Surgeons and Barbers in Edinburgh, I saw a quote from Winifred Rushforth, who started the Davidson Clinic for Family Psychotherapy. She said, '*They will know we are old not by the frailty of the body but by the strength and creativity of the psyche.*' You have a great future ahead of you, sir, and a huge responsibility with this headstrong granddaughter and even a larger role managing our out-of-control world."

Winslow started as if stung. This doctor was closer to the truth than he realized. He knew nothing of his ambition to have a run for senate but seemed to sense it. Much was happening in the life of Winslow Kirk. More than he thought he could handle. He excused himself and wandered off deep in thought.

Dr. Obed remained seated thinking about his own life and future. Willow had just left a group of the girls, and seeing Dr.

Obed sitting alone, she jumped at the chance to chat to him as she had promised.

Dr. Obed was delighted and wasted no time on preliminaries.

"By the way, did you have a chance to examine Dorcas. I mean…"

Willow laughed.

"Look, her so-called boyfriend has gone back to England and a new life. I don't think they were a serious couple. She did confide in me that she felt lonesome at times. Well, we all do, but in her case, it seemed elongated lonesomeness, if you know what I mean."

Dr. Obed nodded. "What should I do?" Obed asked quickly.

Willow looked deep into the doctor's eyes. "She is a very unusual woman, a fitness freak and truly committed to security for her people. Sure, she is no longer a teacher, but she has chosen a very special path. Here's what you will do. Tell her you're still a mission doctor. Tell her you are not signing a contract with Manchester United for millions of dollars. Tell her mission doctors don't get paid a lot of money, you told me less than $200 a month and some months nothing at all. Then tell her you love her and want to marry her."

Obed grabbed a pen. "Let me write this down. What a speech!"

"Don't be ridiculous. Just talk from your heart, Doctor. And don't use a scalpel. Use cotton wool."

Dorcas and Winston sauntered over and joined them.

"What are you two plotting?" Dorcas asked as Obed poured himself some of the freshly made Sipi Falls coffee.

"N-n-n-nothing," the doctor said.

"So lovely that you and Eleanor found each other again after so long," Willow told Winslow.

"It's true," Winslow said. "I feel ten years younger. But she still won't forgive me, you know. Maybe I should come to camp again next year."

"Why not?" Obed laughed. "Why not?"

It was Winslow who spoke next. "You know, I've been thinking of what you said about not trusting anyone. Maybe you could get help from our CIA. I mean, they would be neutral and bring their experience from other countries."

Dorcas shook her head. "I don't think so, sir. They are so far removed from our world, you know. What do they know of us? Have they ever been really hungry like many of these kids?"

"Well, maybe in their training," Winslow suggested.

"I doubt it. The root cause of hunger is poverty, and they have good salaries. They are not poor."

"No, I suppose not," Winslow conceded.

Obed smiled. "She's so right, you know. Your CIA boys know so little of the vile blows and buffets of the world."

It was just at this moment that Eleanor joined the little group.

"Must go and help final packing from the girls' dorm, then say good-bye to the lake," she said. "By the way, those words were mine in *Macbeth* at the Fringe Festival Edinburgh before coming here. I also painted some of the sets. My father thinks I am still there."

"Well, let's hear them," Dorcas said.

"I was the second murderer of Banquo. He had nothing to lose, so he agreed to carry out the murder. It was a small part, but here's what I said." Eleanor strutted center stage.

Winston sat back and basked in the afternoon sun and the youthful enthusiasm of his granddaughter.

> I am one my Liege
> Whom the vile blows and buffets of the world
> Hath so incens'd, that I am reckless
> What I do to spite the world.

Obed clapped his hands.

"Encore," Dorcas shouted. "Encore!"

Eleanor smiled, bowed, and ran off to the dormitories to help with the cleaning.

Dr. Obed took up his argument. "You see, he had nothing to lose. That's the heart of terrorism. Young people who feel they do not belong and so are easily persuaded to take the job of second murderer of Banquo or suicide bomber. Your CIA people don't understand the 'nothing to lose' concept. They don't learn the 'vile blows and buffets of the world' at Harvard or Berkley or Yale and so are not close enough to the suffering of people."

"Exactly right," Dorcas agreed. She took his hand.

The doctor did not move in case the hand should be removed anytime soon. He continued, "And look at us. We are your boots on the ground in Somalia. Our peacekeeping boys are dying there. But we know what's going on because we learn from our boots and not our computers. We have a million refugees from South Sudan in northern camps. Oh, yes, we are close to suffering. Very close."

"Like Ibrahim," Dorcas said.

There was a stunned silence.

Dorcas began to share in the depths of Africa's Great Rift Valley her own thoughts on the world of terror. "Pax Americana is fading, you know. America's retreat from the Middle East is creating a vacuum. As you know nature abhors a vacuum."

"Aristotle."

Winslow, the moneyman, looked in astonishment at Willow. Perhaps he was ready to leave kindergarten and be promoted to first grade.

Dorcas continued, "Correct. And that vacuum today is being filled by Russia and the Islamic Republic of Iran on the one hand and by the adherents of anti-immigrant, anti-NATO far right on the other. We now have the perfect chaos for ISIS and al-Qaeda, now in unison, the perfect hydra to take advantage of."

Now promoted to first grade, Winslow raised his hand.

"Hydra?" Winslow asked. Jeannie Backhouse had said nothing of this. His antennae now finely tuned, he leant forward to listen to this extraordinary woman, this teacher turned spook and Olympic runner.

"In ancient Greek mythology, the Hydra was a serpent-like water beast that possessed more heads than the vase painters could paint. It could not be killed because for each head that was cut off two more would grow. The war on terror is up against the Hydra. For some strange reason we are all hearing the word *Centum the hundred*. I don't know what that indicates, but let's just call it Centum Hydra."

"How do you know so much, Dorcas?" Dr. Obed asked, clearly as impressed as the chairman of the Federal Reserve.

"When you are near, very, very, near, the suffering, you hear many cries and much information," Dorcas told him. "Like Ibrahim."

Dr. Obed wanted this discussion to last, and he ordered some more coffee and sponge cake. The afternoon stretched ahead.

"I shouldn't be talking like this, really, but it's so lovely to have real friends around me," Dorcas said. "You see, several of our officers were killed in the Entebbe bombing. And now a sample of a dirty bomb has been found in men's clothing in Kololo Shopping Mall."

No one interrupted her train of thought. It was too precious for any stray words to stop.

"Personally, I think that al-Qaeda is preparing instructions for its dispersion worldwide with some help of course from the Quds Force, you know, the intelligence unit of Iran's revolutionary guards?"

"America pulled out of the nuclear deal we had with Iran," Dr. Obed said.

"Stop blaming the US," Winslow objected. "We're all in this together. What a strange and hostile world we live in now. I'll just be glad to get my granddaughter back home safely. Maybe even with visits to Washington if I decide to run for senator."

Dorcas put down her cup of coffee. She then stood up. Her body began to shake. "You're kidding me! You've got to be kidding me!" she shouted.

"What so bad about that?"

"Oh, dear God!" Dorcas walked round in a few circles. "He is chair of the Federal Reserve?"

"Yes, that's right," Willow said.

"And he may run for senator?"

Winslow nodded.

"And his granddaughter arrived just after the Entebbe bombing. And you were warned in Basle!"

"Dorcas, what's wrong!" Dr. Obed took her hand and pushed her back into the camp chair.

"What's wrong, Dorcas?" Winslow asked. "Tell us."

For some time the teacher turned military intelligence officer was silent. She looked up at the sky and then at her friends.

"Ibrahim may tell us more when he feels better. But in the last hour, we have received intel as to what happened in your drone strike in Somalia. Abu escaped. But do you know who was killed?"

Winslow shook his head.

"A teenage girl. A daughter of Abu. His only child. Her name is Fatima, age seventeen. Four other young people also died. It seems that the chip to help the drone locate him had been put in his Koran. Her father gave it to his daughter to look after when he went out in search of a new source of water for the village. Terrible drought here in East Africa now, you know."

Winslow began quoting the text he had received in Basle. "An eye for an eye."

Dorcas nodded. "It's a real threat. It refers to an ancient blood feud which would stop conflict between tribes. One person's death, like Abu's granddaughter, can be atoned for by the death of another. The tyrant wants revenge."

"Dear God," Willow almost whispered. She then continued, "Though tyrants threat, though Lyons rage and roar."

"Pardon?" Dorcas asked.

"Oh, nothing, just an old poem," Willow said. "Scotland's first female poet to be published. Lady Culross. She wrote 'Aine Godly Dreame.'"

"Though tyrants threat, though Lyons rage and roar." Dorcas shook her head. "Oh, it's much worse. Listen, the prophet Muhammad's daughter was also called Fatima. He was so close to his daughter that he said, 'Fatima is part of my body; whoever hurts her hurts me; and whoever has hurt me has hurt God.' You see, blood feud is one of the concepts of Sharia Law. It is hard for us to understand, but the family honor can only be cleansed by the slaying of a member of the offender's family. Abu is now duty bound to kill the Chairman's granddaughter, Eleanor."

Winslow rubbed his eyes. A deep sense of foreboding shrouded him. The ancient Rift Valley had never seemed so silent. Three Uganda kob stood like statues unmoving. Two crested cranes stopped bobbing their colorful crowns. The sun seemed to stop in her splendor valley.

Dorcas jumped up again. "I'll get a Ugandan army chopper to take you and Eleanor to Entebbe and out on the next international flight."

Winslow said he would immediately call Jeannie Backhouse, the secretary of state, with this new intelligence. They all raced toward the dormitories.

"Eleanor!" Winslow yelled. "Eleanor!"

Dorcas outran them and arrived first.

Three girls were packing up and looked up at the frantic visitors.

"Where is Eleanor?" Dorcas demanded.

"She went with Kiabo to say good-bye to the lake," little Rose told them.

"God, no," Dorcas groaned.

Back at the deserted chairs, Winston's briefcase had fallen. The manuscript fell out opened at this page. An omen?

*****

FLORENZ

You know, Richarn, we have good relations with the chiefs
and the people we meet on the way. It is the traders and
slavers who are turning each area they visit into a wasp's nest.
Sam showed me a quote from David Livingstone's diary
quoted in *The Times*. He said, "The strangest disease I Have

seen in Africa seems really to be broken-heartedness and it attacks free men who have been captured and made slaves."

SAATHORN

RICHARN

It is true, madame. The broken heart is a bad sickness. The slavers steal cattle, they steal people to sell them in Khartoum. They also sell the cattle for ivory to take back to Khartoum. Bad people.

As they move from camp they see a caravan of over fifty slaves all in wooden nooses. Florence and Richarn hide behind some bushes. Moosa Pasha Hamdi, who had bid for Florence in Viddin, is leading them.

HAMDI

(snarling with whip in hand)

Faster, faster, I need you all in the markets of Kharoum before the beginning of the fast of Ramadan.

As the pace quickens a small slave boy falls and his small body slips under the noose. He rushes away toward the bushes where / Florence and Richarn are concealed.

SAAT

Salaam, madame! Take me, help me. I am Saat.

FLORENZ

(tears in her eyes as she remembers Ali in Viddin)

Slave boy, I was once a slave. Quick. Richarn, take him back to camp now.

Richarn rushes off with the little slave boy, Saat. Florence remains transfixed with horror. Moosa Pasha Hamdi comes crashing through the bush followed by his deputy Sultan Hamed.

PASHA MUSA HAMDI

Florence and Hamdi recognize each other. This is the major crisis point of the movie. Florence's face sags, and she loses all her sprit.

FLORENZ

No, please no. I am betrothed. My husband is Baker Pasha.

PASHA MUSA HAMDI

But he is not here. Allah be praised. I bought
you. Baker Pasha stole you, and now you are
rightfully mine again. Guards, seize her!
Guards put Florence into Saat's wooden slave chain. The
caravan moves north.

Chapter

13

Lake Albert was always dotted with fishing boats. Part of the livelihood of so many people clinging to the lakeside, they also formed an enchanting scene at night when they used little lamps to do their illegal fishing for small *kapenta* by light, luring their catch into their nets. Many of the fishermen knew each other, but there were also others from Congo who fed from this secondary source of the river Nile.

Eleanor and Kiabo held hands and spoke together.

"Good-bye, sweet lake. Good-bye, Camp Hopeful. Good-bye, dear friends."

One of the fishing boats bobbed into the pebbles of the shoreline, and a couple of fishermen beckoned them over. They walked toward the boat and gasped at the full catch of fish.

"Well done," Eleanor said.

Without warning strong hands grabbed the girls and deposited them among the fish catch.

"Get off. No, no, no," Kiabo screamed. "Never, never, never again!" All the hurts of the past flooded over. She clung to Eleanor. "Don't leave me," she begged. "Ever."

The fake fishermen ignored her and swiftly rowed furiously out into the lake. Kiabo looked up and stared into the eyes of the Entebbe bomber. Once again her young life was plunged into chaos on Lake Albert.

"Bravo, *mes amis*, bravo," they told each other. "Al-Shabaab will now pay us the balance due."

Like Somali pirates who had terrorized cargo and passenger vessels for years, the remnant of the coltan mine guards were now in need of cash replenishment. Darkness was falling. The men sang to mask the groan of the girls. After half an hour of swift rowing, they came close to a little island facing a bay into Congo. Unlike the regular fishermen who knew the vagaries and dangers of the lake, they had no fear. This was clearly a mistake.

*****

Willow followed Winslow and Dorcas as they sprinted down to the lake. Some women were preparing fish for market some distance from shore.

"Two girls, one black one white?"

The women shook their heads. Dorcas rushed to a little fishing boat that was being pulled up the pebbled beach. The fishermen indicated that, yes, two girls had gone off quickly in another boat, and they pointed vaguely in the direction to the west to Congo. Dorcas screamed into her phone, and within fifteen minutes, a military motor launch *M. V. Rwenzori* arrived. With engines already running was a brand-new thirty-foot Pursuit OS 315 patrol boat. This boat was powered by two Yamaha three-hundred-horsepower four-stroke engines that enabled a top speed of fifty miles per hour. Two of these were already south in Lake Victoria, and this one had recently been placed in the small bay below the Masindi Sugar Factory and Plantation. Col. Ben Tumusiime and Col. Sam Mulindwa were in charge. Maj. A. B. Mbonye assisted.

Introductions were done quickly then Dorcas, Willow, and Winslow clambered aboard. No one seemed to notice that Ibrahim, who had arrived at the lake now, went onboard with them. Col. Ben Tumusiime's English accent was a mix of Uganda Broadcasting Corporation and England's Sandhurst Military College. As well as Col. Tumusiime's two brothers, Col. Sam

Mulindwa had also lost one brother in Somalia and they were in very foul moods. Col. Tumusiime spoke to Winslow.

"Real sorry, sir. This is our situation here in Uganda now. Terror of al-Shabaab and also the idiot genocidaires from Congo after their mines were closed down. Don't worry, we'll find the girls. If it's only the Congo boys, there will be a ransom note soon enough." He looked west to the last of the setting sun's crimson streaks, the darkening sky and the Democratic Republic of Congo. "Problem is, light is going swiftly."

Winslow made a call to the US ambassador in Kampala and to the secretary of state.

"The ambassador will ask the Navy SEALs to come ASAP from Juba. He has sent the Tilt Rotor up for them."

"Must move swiftly, sir," Col. Sam said. "Our patrol boat and crew are ready to set off now." He pointed out over the darkening lake.

"Yes, of course, let's go."

*****

By the time the little fishing craft was nearing the island, Eleanor and Kiabo were subdued and were clinging to each other among the fish catch. Most hippos had already left the lake to begin their nightly search for their eighty pounds of grass on shore. But one older male approaching his allotted life span of forty years was in no particular rush. Already submerged for five minutes, he rose gently to the surface, and to the consternation of the genocidaires, his four-ton frame lifted the boat clear out of the water. The fake fishermen looked in horror at the blood-red hulk under them. This was not sweat or blood, but the oily red substance hippos emit as a skin moistener and sunblock, which also provides protection against germs. Widower hippo shook off the strange intrusion to his nightly feed and made his way ashore. The canoe plunged into the darkening waters of the lake.

"Can you swim?" Eleanor yelled.

"No," Kiabo spluttered.

For most of her young life, Eleanor had been carefully looked after, driven around, helped with whatever she needed. Now suddenly she was alone and in charge. Adrenaline pumped through her. *Well, thank God for all these swimming galas I've taken part in*, she thought. She circled around 360 degrees and spotted what seemed to be the nearest island away from any dangerous hippos and the spluttering thugs for hire.

"Kiabo, hold my back and kick your feet behind you," she yelled as she began to swim to safety. She looked back at the genocidaires who were struggling in the water. Swimming was not one of their strong suits and several other hippos were wading toward them in the shallows. The little fishing boat sank beneath the black lake.

A flock of cormorants flew over them, followed by some maribou storks, the nemesis of aircraft takeoffs from Entebbe airport.

"Daylight almost gone, and then we're sunk literally," Eleanor spluttered. "Get away from the hippos and the hijackers." She swam in the opposite direction.

Kiabo was still coughing water and did not reply. She obediently clung to Eleanor's back, making sure her head was resting above the waters. Eleanor began her swim and then encountered two problems. First of all, the tide seemed to be moving toward her, thus making her movement to the island more difficult. The second problem was that, although the lake had looked calm from the air, there were in fact waves that were more than a foot high. As she pulled away from the place where the fishing boat had sunk, she focused on her breathing.

Eleanor was a strong swimmer, but the present circumstances were far from ideal. She kicked off her shoes and began to adapt her breathing to when she emerged from each of the waves. Her stroke was a simple breaststroke. Kiabo's weight and frantic movements were holding her back. *Don't think we're going to make it*, she thought. The little island looked very far away. She turned to see how Kiabo was doing and saw a very frightened face staring back at her. As she turned her head to face the next wave, something solid hit her. Then an arm fell onto her right shoulder.

"Get off, Kiabo!" she yelled. She held the arm, looked back, and saw that it was black but not Kiabo's.

Eleanor screamed. She pushed the arm away and then saw the rest of the body bobbing beside her. It was one of the hijackers, and he was already dead. Dropping the arm, Eleanor kept swimming. The next obstacle she encountered was more useful. She put up her right hand and grabbed it. She saw an empty wooden crate with large letters on the side, "Bell Beer."

"Kiabo, hold on to this!" she yelled. Eleanor then took the other side of the crate, and together, they pushed it forward into the waves. It was perhaps a slight improvement, but their progress remained painfully slow. The sun was almost beyond the western horizon, and the lake was darkening.

In these darkening waters of Lake Albert, Eleanor matured. With the realization that she alone could save her new friend, Kiabo, and herself, her self-confidence grew. "Plus et en vous," the motto of Gordonstoun School in Scotland where she had attended a summer school. There's more in you than you think. Hidden depths, until now unknown to her or her parents, were revealed like the flotsam on the lake.

"Hold on to the crate, Kiabo!" she yelled as she struck out for the island. "And keep your mouth shut. You're swallowing too much water!" Like the final push in her high school swimming gala, she felt adrenaline pump through her. But was there enough to last the distance? The waves seemed to be rising higher, the light breeze was now a strong wind and, unfortunately, blowing from the island into their faces. Just ahead Eleanor saw a protruding black rock.

"Let's rest here for a few minutes!" she yelled. "But keep hold of the beer crate."

She pulled herself up onto the flat surface and gratefully sucked in lungful of air. As she lay there with her head resting on the volcanic surface, she saw two beetles nonchalantly meandering over the rock. Each had identical multicolored shells—red, tea green, and banana yellow. Their centerpiece was a black pentagon. Eleanor stared transfixed. Despite the precariousness of their situation, she could not help but marvel at such beauty. Kiabo clung to the beer crate but also spotted the insects.

"You see I told you, Princess Eleanor, that I would show you wonderful hidden things in Africa!" she yelled.

Eleanor plopped back into the lake and pulled her friend behind her.

"The only wonder I want to see now is a real island, dry, dry land," she spluttered.

The red ball of the sun was bowing beyond the horizon, signaling to all who saw her on the African equator that darkness— real black, no-electricity blackness—would soon engulf their world. Eleanor was now quite frantic. She was sure they could not make landfall before darkness but could not tell her friend for fear of creating risky panic. Her arms were weary; and Kiabo, despite the beer crate, seemed heavier than ever. A curious cormorant flew wave-high over them. Then suddenly help came from an unexpected quarter.

"*Ssebo!*" It was Kiabo who spotted it first.

A small fishing boat off to their port side with four men paddling the craft away from the island in preparation for their night's fishing. Small kerosene Tillich lamps hung from the sides.

"*Ssebo!* Help!"

At first the men didn't seem to notice them and kept their steady paddling rhythm. They were now pulling away from the girls.

"Together, Princess, together. One, two, three, ssebo."

So together they screamed, and one of the fishermen looked back.

"They're coming back. Thank God they're coming back," Eleanor said. "What did we yell anyway?"

Kiabo grinned. "In our language, it means a kind of respectful address to a man. Something like *sir*," she explained.

The boat had bright-colored markings and just one word painted on the starboard bow, "Anyway." Kiabo yelled at the fishermen and explained to them in Luganda what had happened.

"Al-Shabaab?" one of them asked. "Too bad, too very bad!"

The girls were pulled into the boat. It stank of fish although none had yet been caught.

"Uncle Julius!" Kiabo yelled as she recognized one of the men. "Eleanor, this must be my island. Jjaja will be here."

"Who?"

"My auntie Bella," Kiabo said with a grin. "My dear auntie. Granny Maud's sister. We're safe, very safe!"

The fishermen were now arguing as to what had happened to the girls. Eleanor explained about the fishermen.

"Al-Shabaab," Julius said. "Since our soldiers are peacekeepers in Somalia, they truly hate us. They are still after us. Wicked people."

"Auntie, auntie!" Kiabo yelled.

Eleanor looked out of the canoe and saw in the now almost dark evening a small gnarled woman grinning at them and showing her lack of teeth. The fishermen lifted the two girls out onto the pebbly shore. Old pieces of net, fish heads, and plastic bottles littered it. Kiabo ran into her aunt's outstretched arms.

"Eleanor, this is my auntie," she said.

Eleanor grinned and then felt the warm but bony embrace of the old lady. "Imagine out of all these islands in Lake Albert, we found yours!" Eleanor said.

"What a coincidence!"

Meanwhile, Auntie just could not stop speaking.

"What's she saying?" Eleanor asked.

"She says she saw the fishermen land by chopper on the north of her island and then steal a fishing boat already fish-full. Our men were heading out after them. She says please give her our wet clothes and she will help us with something else."

"Did the helicopter take off again, Auntie?" Kiabo asked. An incisive and critical question.

"I don't know," Grannie's sister replied.

Soon the girls were sitting around a little fire drinking sweet tea. Eleanor laughed as she looked down at the dress Auntie had put on her. It had seen so many washings that the flowers on it were faded. She looked at bare threads freeing themselves from the rest of the garment. In a matter of hours one of the world's richest girls was now looking more like a waif and stray. Eleanor's first thought was for communication. Her iPhone was gone somewhere deep in Lake Albert.

"Kiabo, please ask if anyone has a cell phone," she said.

Auntie understood the request and began talking again incessantly. Eleanor raised her eyebrows to Kiabo.

"She says no problem, my uncle Kiwanuka, the head man of the island, has one and a solar charger so it can be kept alive by the sun. She says we are very modern here like New York!"

"Can I use it now to call my grandfather?" she asked.

Kiabo and Auntie were silent.

"Well, can I?"

Kiabo gave the simple reply. "No," she said.

"Why not?"

"There's no network on this island," Kiabo said simply.

"Then what's the point of having a phone," Eleanor spluttered. "Where is there network?"

Auntie started talking again.

"She says there is network in the papyrus where the ancient prehistoric birds nest."

"Well, what are we waiting for? Let's go there now," Eleanor shouted.

Again there was a silence.

Then Kiabo said one more time, "No."

Eleanor slumped forward defeated. "Why?" she whispered. "Why?"

"My uncle says there are schools of hippos beside the place of the ancient birds. Last week one of the fishermen died when his canoe was overturned by the hippos. Too dangerous at dusk, but we can go in one hour when they are all out of the water on land."

This was certainly not the response Eleanor wanted to hear. Jajja cooked them some fish and then took the girls into a small hut. Eleanor was given a very thin blanket, and she lay down on a mat on the floor. A light breeze blew off the lake, and it was pleasantly warm in the hut. Eleanor thought she would never sleep but was surprised that after a brief discussion with Kiabo she did doze.

*****

She was back in Connecticut holding pink teddy.

"Grandpa, what will pink teddy get from Santa?"

Her grandfather smiled and shook his head like an Indian shopkeeper discussing the price of chickpeas.

"A secret, Eleanor, a secret. You wait and see. Answers don't always come right away, you know. Sometimes we need to wait."

*****

She woke with a start. *I must call Grandpa now now, now.* All thought of patience was gone.

As the moon was arcing over the lake, Mr. Kiwanuka and a few other fishermen began to launch their canoe.

"Why don't you have a motor on this?" Eleanor asked.

The fishermen paddled furiously.

The youngest one, a twin called Wasswa, replied, "We did have a Yamaha motor, which we borrowed from a police motorcycle in Masindi. But it was stolen a few nights ago. We suspect the owner of the motorcycle."

Slowly, they paddled away. As they left shore, Eleanor asked Kiabo, "What are these ancient birds anyway?"

"Very rare and many tourists come from Europe to see them."

As they reached the papyrus, Eleanor could see patches of purple flowers from the invasive lake hyacinth and beyond them a large nest with the strangest bird she had ever set eyes on. A large gray bird and the bill resembling a shoe.

"Shoebill stork," Kiabo whispered. "We are now in their breeding grounds. Network is often very good from here."

"So the birds can call home." Eleanor grinned.

Mr. Kiwanuka gave her his mobile phone.

"But I don't know Grandpa's number. It's on my iPhone," she said.

Kiabo grinned. "Lucky I have my memory card right here," she said, tapping her forehead. "It's +12035717777."

Eleanor quickly typed it into the little Nokia phone.

A prehistoric shoebill stork waddled off her nest and peered at this modern marvel.

*****

Meanwhile, aboard *M.V. Rwenzori* the atmosphere was frantic.

Dr. Obed Ochola clung to Dorcas. Winslow clung to Willow. Col. Mulindwa told himself for the umpteenth time that taking civilians on this mission was nuts. Too much emotional baggage. They had already searched a couple of small islands and were close to giving up when Winslow's phone rang.

"Eleanor!" he shouted. "Where are you?"

Eleanor gave their location and said they were now making their way back to Auntie Bella's island.

"Good news!" Winslow told everyone onboard.

They are paddling now back to Buvuma Island. The speed launch captain set his GPS, and they sped off.

"What a relief," muttered Willow. "Wonder how they escaped? Kiabo and your granddaughter are quite a pair."

Ibrahim sat immobile up in the bows of the launch listening, ever listening.

Col. Sam Mulindwa, Col. Ted Tumusiime, and Maj. J. B. Mbonye were fully armed with Bushmaster XM15 rifles, the ones used in the killing of the children at Sandy Hook Elementary

School in Connecticut, but these were adapted with full automatic rather than semiautomatic function.

Col. Tumusiime gave the orders. "Buvuma Island immediately. Full steam ahead! Keep the searchlights circling. Keep checking all fishing boats in the vicinity. ETA, eight minutes. Soon be there."

"So many small lights from fishing boats. Seems a strange time to go fishing in the dead of night. What are they up to?"

Col. Sam smiled. "Illegal fishing really, very common on Lake Albert. They use kerosene lamps to attract small fish, *kapenta*, to the surface and then net them."

"So why not stop it?" Willow asked.

Col. Sam guffawed with laughter and held his ample sides.

"As Charles Dickens said, 'The law is an ass,' and here on remote parts of the lakes, the long arm of the law is rather short. The real problem is that this night fishing is making our task of locating a terrorist canoe almost impossible. Like looking for a needle in the proverbial haystack."

Winslow's spirits plummeted, then lifted with the crescent moon rising above them. "Eleanor lass, we're coming," he told the night.

Chapter

14

The Ugandan Army launch reached Buvuma Island in just under eight minutes.

Col. Ben Tumusiime gave orders, and they pulled up alongside a little makeshift pier that had seen better days.

Winslow and Willow looked ashore and then at each other.

"Eleanor, Entebbe Airport, home," Winslow muttered.

Willow looked into his exhausted features. "Agreed," she whispered.

It was Dorcas who spoke first, not really a voice, more an anguished croak.

"Oh God, no, no, no, no!" she screamed.

Lying on the pebbled beach were the lifeless bodies of two of the fishermen who had rescued the girls. Then they heard the wailing from further up the beach at the settlement of small huts. They ran toward them.

Dorcas arrived first and held the shoulders of one woman, who was ululating and weeping all at the same time.

"What happened, Auntie Bella?"

In a torrent of Luganda the story came out. Blood streamed from her forehead.

"What does she say?" Willow asked.

Dorcas slumped forward. "God, please, not again," she muttered to herself. Then she straightened up and addressed the others. "She said Kiabo and Eleanor had just arrived back with our fishermen when three men came at the same time from where the chopper had landed. They killed Paul and Julius and took Kiabo and Eleanor with them. They were not the Rwandans who took the canoe. They were Somalis."

"And you?" Col. Sam asked Auntie Bella.

"I ran over and tried to stop them. They are wicked. My head, it is broken."

"Which direction did they take?" Col. Sam asked.

Several women pointed in a series of contradictory directions. Hopeless.

Col. Sam ordered his team to search the island.

In the midst of this mayhem, Ibrahim disappeared.

Then there was the sound of a helicopter preparing for takeoff. The Ugandan soldiers led the charge to the north end of the little island. As they arrived they saw the Russian built MI-24 helicopter with whirring wings take off.

"Shoot it down!" Maj. A. B. Mbonye screamed.

Dorcas pushed his gun down. "No, the girls are onboard."

They all watched helplessly as the chopper headed directly northwest into Congo.

"Ibrahim!" It was Dorcas who saw him first. He was lying face down in the muddy makeshift landing pad of the helicopter. "Ibrahim." She lifted his head.

Ibrahim opened one eye, rubbed his bruised head, then passed out.

Dorcas cradled him in her arms.

Col. Tumusiime moaned, "A needle in a haystack is a walk in the playground compared to looking for a person in Congo."

With these words dragging all hearts down, they made their way back to Camp Hopeful, taking with them the corpses of the two fishermen and a very dazed Ibrahim.

*****

That night Dorcas, Dr. Ochola, and Willow sat in silence looking over Lake Albert. The mood was somber. Flashes of lightning lit up the little fishing boats on the lake followed by rumbles of thunder. Winslow without a word left the group and retired to his room. He sat alone. He opened up some notes of his grandfather. As he read, the dam burst. He wept.

Thunder rumbled over the lake.

"Eleanor! God, no, no, no! I cannot face Mother with this."

Tears coursed down his cheeks in rivulets. His shoulders shook in unison with the thunder claps. He stared out into the bleak dusk, bleak like his soul, bleak like his spirit, bleak like his own lonely future. Then he read his grandfather's words.

"A study which may seem rather dry and academic a study of the medieval mystics but now it mirrors my own soul tonight. This talk of 'the dark night of the soul' is real. Why did my laddie walk into Long Island Sound? Why? Why? St. John of the Cross's sixteenth century writing says 'Aridity, lost on the road, abandoned by God, losing the spirit of tranquility and peace, all spiritual blessing is over.' That's me. Me."

Winslow nodded. "Me too, Grandpa, me too," he muttered to a gecko clinging to the wall of his room.

Outside the room, Willow clung to her manuscript as if willing it to speak and offer some comfort. Without knocking, she slowly entered the room and sat down on a large armchair. Winslow was slumped stretched out on a sofa.

"If you wish to be alone, kick me out now. Otherwise, I'm just here to share the silence and listen if you like."

Winslow started speaking as if to the wall or the lake or the black African night.

"Willow, there's something else I didn't share. Something I've shared with no other person."

"Deep secrets, eh? We all have these for sure."

"Mmm. The night after my father walked into Long Island Sound, I had a dream. I saw the island Pequot about half a mile from shore where we often boated for picnics and fun. My father was standing there waving me over. When I woke, I threw on shorts and a T-shirt and took my kayak out to it. There I found, I found…"

Willow stood up and sat down on the sofa. She put her arm around Winslow and kissed him on the cheek.

Winslow shuddered, then continued, "He was floating. I put a line round him and pulled him home to the beach near us. The longest, hardest journey I've ever done. I put the kayak away and went and told my mother that Daddy had washed up."

In the ensuing silence, Winslow glanced at the manuscript. "You never seem to be without it, do you?" Winslow took it and opened it.

They both stared at the script.

Then Winslow spoke. "So how did Florence, the slave girl, escape? At least this screenplay seems to have a happy ending." Winslow took the manuscript from her.

*****

FULL SHOT. LITTLE SAAT HAS GRABBED SAM'S RIFLE FROM RICHARN AND IS HOLDING IT. – AFTERNOON
SAAT
Siit has been captured. We must go after her!
RICHARN
Are you mad! We have nothing! They have the soldiers.
SAAT
I have an idea.
In Acholi with English subtitles.
(he whispers to Richarn)

They both run ahead of the slavers and hide. Saat points out to Richarn huge hives of wild bees in the trees. As the slaver party walks underneath, Saat grabs Richarn's gun called the Baby and fires at the nests. Total confusion ensues. The bees swarm and begin to attack the slavers, who run screaming. Saat is thrown backward at the report. He get up and runs toward Florence and

142

frees her. Richarn frees other slaves. Saat and Richarn run off into the woods. Saat is quite badly bitten but doesn't seem to notice.

SAAT (CONT'D)
(yells at other slaves in Acholi)
Go homee, go homee!

Florence yells to Saat and Richarn.

FLORENZ
Quick, quick, to look for Baker Pasha!

Rush through undergrowth. After a long march, it is now toward evening and they hear sounds.

FLORENZ (CONT'D)
Listen! Listen! It is Sam.

Sounds of groans come from undergrowth. They come to a clearing and see a wounded buffalo preparing to run at Sam, who is on the ground.

FLORENZ (CONT'D)
The gun, give me the gun, quick.

Richarn hands the gun over to Florence. She takes aim and fires, but it is now empty.

FLORENZ (CONT'D)
Oh, God, help me.

Saat picks up pebbles and feeds them into the gun. He takes aim and fires at the buffalo as it charges Sam. The stones divert it, and it charges Saat. He rushes off and runs behind a huge boulder. The buffalo hits the boulder and then wanders off in a raging haze.

FLORENZ (CONT'D)
Sam, Sam, are you all right?
(she rushes over to him and helps him up)

SAMUEL BAKER
In the nick of time, old girl. Well done! Who
the devil is that impish black boy?

FLORENZ
It's a long story. His name is Saat. Come back to camp and
hear the whole terrible tale. I'm afraid, Sam, very afraid. I
thought I was free forever, but now I know I can never be free.

They make their way back to camp. Sit outside and share their adventures together.

FLORENZ (CONT'D)
Saat, bring Baker Pasha some whiskey.
SAMUEL BAKER
Whiskey?
FLORENZ
Well, you had made the still and were wondering what to distill in it. When you were gone I found the answer.
SAMUEL BAKER
Morning noon and night you amaze me, Flori. All right, what is the answer?
FLORENZ
Sometimes the answer is right under your very nose. When you were gone, Chief Katchiba brought us many sweet potatoes, and we have been enjoying them. I used the excess to make your whiskey. It may not be the dram you dream about from Scotland from Glen Tilt, but there's plenty of it.
SAAT
(sips the whiskey)
Mmm. Not bad at all. Please have some yourself.
It may keep the mal aire, the malaria, away.

They drink in silence. Saat sits nearby, putting green leaves on his bee stings.

*****

"Did it happen like that?"

Willow smiled. "Well, the screenplay says based on a true story, which means it has some of my, shall we say, embellishments."

"But Florence and Sam triumphed together?"

"That they did," Willow whispered. "That they did."

The rest of the night Winslow and Willow shared the sadness of defeat snoozing, waking, snoozing.

One moment when he was awake, he watched Willow's steady breathing and picked up Robert Kirk's strange treatise, *The Secret Commonwealth of Elves, Fauns and Fairies*. The chairman of the Federal Reserve (acting, acting) had come a long way from his own tome *Money Matters*!

> The sagacious Scots are favored by several visions and predictions, by surprises and raptures which often foretell the future. To which purpose the learned lynx-eyed Mr. Baxter on Revelation 12 vs 7, writing of the fight betwixt Michael and the Dragon, gives a very pertinent note, viz. that he knows not but ere any great action (especially *tragical*) is done on earth, that first the battle and victory is acted and achieved in the air betwixt the good and evil spirits.

The little book fell from his grasp as Winslow fell into a deep sleep.

*****

Winslow saw clearly the good spirits but was sad to see how weak they seemed. Ibrahim held hands with Kiabo's ancient grandmother, Maud, as they smiled at each other floating past him. He grimaced as he saw the marks of torture on Ibrahim's arms and brow and Granny's care-worn face. Then in a flash, he saw on the shores of St. Andrews in high summer his own grandfather.

"Breathe, laddie, breathe. That's what His Majesty's Royal Navy taught us. Now time me from when I submerge."

The stopwatch was handed to Winslow as his grandfather waded out into the chilly water of the North Sea and then disappeared underwater. One minute passed. Winslow walked up and down the beach, then back to the spot where his grandfather had gone under. Two minutes passed, and he truly panicked. He began to run for help when suddenly at two minutes and ten seconds the head of his grandfather popped up above the waves.

"Now you do it," he commanded.

Winslow waded out to sea, took as deep a breath as he could, then submerged.

"One minute. Not bad, lad. Just keep practicing."

Darkening clouds threatened a serious storm. Winslow watched as his grandfather glowed brighter and brighter as he was swept into the skies. The dark clouds melted like snowflakes on a river until all he saw was blinding light.

*****

"Too bright. Sore even!" Winslow sat up and rubbed his eyes.

"A nightmare?" Willow asked.

Winslow did not reply.

His new pearl of faith and mystery was to be severely tested. *Must the battle for victory really begin in heaven between evil and good spirits?* he wondered. He did not know that oysters themselves from which the pearl sometimes emerges lead a dreadful but exciting life full of stress, passion, and danger. The Romans loved them and were sure it was the reason for their large families. Aphrodisiac indeed. Oysters are survivors. Oysters are only as good as the waters that feed them. Oysters need fresh water from a river-feeding the sea. Oysters live precarious lives. Oysters' eggs are devoured by millions of other sea creatures. If Winslow had known all this, he would have realized that his incipient faith was about to be severely tested.

Part 3

Chapter

15

As first hints of light tinged the eastern sky, one sound on the roof of the oil drillers' hut brought Willow and Winslow fully awake. More urgent, more strident than any alarm clock, the squawk of several guinea fowl made them both sit upright.

"What the hell's that?" Winslow asked.

Willow laughed. "Guinea fowl. Their mini eggs are delicious for breakfast, don't you know?"

The guinea fowl ruckus was followed by urgent knocking on Winslow's door.

"Sir, come quickly. We have some new intelligence."

After showers, Willow and Winslow joined the Ugandan army and Ibrahim in the dining hall of the oil drillers' camp.

Over breakfast Dorcas shared what they had put together during the night.

"Ibrahim is amazing. Part of his mission in Somalia was to track al-Shabaab helicopters by putting GPS trackers under them. That's how he was captured. He had hid his little pouch with GPS and then when he escaped, he dug it up again. Wouldn't let it go for all the world."

"What are they?" Winslow asked.

"Looks like a lipstick. Small, about two inches. He put a GL300 real-time GPS tracker under the MI-17 military chopper before it took off. From the moment of his activation, battery life is two weeks. We have tracked it. It landed and took off again so probably dropped Eleanor and Kiabo there."

"Where?" Willow and Winslow spoke together.

Like the African sun's rose-red fingers now breaking over the eastern horizon of Lake Albert, a glimmer of hope dawned in Winslow's soul.

Dorcas was silent for a moment.

"Well, the good news is that we have tracked it. The bad news is where it landed."

Winslow's eyes asked the question again. "Where?"

"Ituri Forest. Perhaps the world's last true wilderness. Remote, dense, ungoverned."

"You know the place?"

"Yes and no. I went to the outskirts with the Ugandan army when Kiabo was abducted and taken there. But only one man actually went in and brought her safely out."

"It wouldn't be Ibrahim again?" Willow's admiration for poor, bruised Ibrahim was growing.

"The very one. I went with him as he entered and brought him out again, but the rest of the time he was alone." Dorcas looked very thoughtful. "For several days we left him alone in the forest. Later he told us how he had been helped by a forest pygmy called Kaluki. He even learned some of his language. Ibrahim is beyond smart, you know.

"I suggest that we now send our own military only reconnaissance mission to Ituri. I'll call a military helicopter now. No civilians."

Winslow stood up. "I'm coming. I won't get in your way, I promise."

"Me too," Willow said.

Winslow looked at her. "You?"

"Yes, me too. Camp Hopeful just wouldn't be the same without Kiabo and Eleanor."

As they were speaking, a Ugandan helicopter appeared and landed on the Camp Hopeful soccer pitch. As the Ugandan soldiers, plus Willow and Winslow, clambered in, no one seemed to notice that Ibrahim also quietly made his way up the shaking steps. Col. Ben Tumusiime and Maj. Dorcas seemed far from happy with this arrangement but reluctantly agreed. The moneyman's African odyssey continued into its final wilderness.

*****

In DR Congo, a country the size of Western Europe, with few paved roads there, lies in a remote part on the northeast corner a true wilderness called Ituri Forest.

Deep in that forest Kaluki sat trancelike, in a kind of innocent wonderment, on the mud floor, his gaze fixed on the cave wall. From the beginning of time his security and that of his people had depended simply on trust—trust based on empathy, cooperation, and good relations. Now that trust was broken completely with the arrival of new peoples so very strange to him and his people, so terrifying. Parts of the forest had been cleared for the arrival and takeoff of the white man's bird. He had seen this creature before in the skies but never in his forest.

In his cave, red stick figures carrying what looked like clubs were chasing a buffalo, a deer, a monkey. Kaluki smiled. *Just like us today*, he thought. He slowly turned his head to the left and stopped as he saw a series of blue concentric circles. Twitching his large flat nose, he puzzled over these for a long period of what people in the busy chaotic world call time. A mystery, he told himself. He stared at the repetitive patterns. Then his eyes converged near their middle. Suddenly, striking stereoscopic illusions appeared. He stopped thinking about the meaning and gave himself up to the 3D movement. His mouth opened in surprise and delight.

Kaluki had seen many years. He was a kind, gentle, and thoughtful man; but his circle of loyalties was now narrowing dramatically. The movable pygmy villages of the Efe people had, over the years, enjoyed reasonable relations with those they called animals or savages, large black tribesmen outside the forest. Of course, the BaNgwana, who cultivated crops and kept cattle on their land outside the Ituri Forest, said the same about the pygmy peoples. But over the years they had traded animal skins for tobacco, honeycombs for metal spearheads, and had generally been understanding neighbors. But now everything had changed with the arrival of strange, new, and violent people, some said even from beyond Africa herself. His perfect safe haven over centuries was now to become a new safe haven for these strangers. As a good philosopher, Kaluki allowed his mind to wander from the problem and return from a different direction. He continued to stare unblinking at the stone wall. Rock art, the common heritage of all mankind. He knew that the ancestors in the blue concentric circles had a sign for him, but his mind and imagination was unable to open it. Deciding to come back to the problem at a later time, he stood and left the cave. He pushed through thick interwoven vines and branches that obscured the cave's entrance from view. From the cave entrance he looked down onto the home of his people, the forest canopy, huge trees all seeking light. His eyes were drawn to what looked like several honeybees.

Kaluki smacked his lips at the thought of some sweet wild honey. In shock from the recent disaster, his metabolism longed for this more than anything. But when he looked closer he saw that the bees were, in fact, flowers growing in one of the tree branches. These bee-like exotic orchids sparkled in the sun. A lone tea-green butterfly alighted on one of the flowers. Seconds later she was chased off by a real bee.

Unaware of the orchid's sexual trickery to ensure efficient pollination, he crawled into the orchid's heart. Kaluki watched carefully as the bee emerged and flew off. *Probably a hive nearby*, he thought and went in search of it. En route, he walked effortlessly down into the thicker forest and on the way paused to harvest some deadly nightshade from which he would extract the deadly poison for hunting. This poison is so deadly that a large antelope shot with a single bone-tipped arrow dipped in the mixture would be dead within hours. On the way he picked some fluffy pink mushrooms and stored them in his little black-and-white colobus monkey skin pouch. If hunting was successful, he would add these to the meat stew. He smacked his large lips as he thought of the crackling from the skin of the giant warthog and the succulent juices of the meat.

Then he saw the hives high in the treetops. He had neither the will nor the energy to climb high into the forest canopy. *When you are old like me*, he thought, *you have to find new ways to achieve the same results.* Of course, he knew the reputation of the wild African bee, the most deadly and aggressive of all bees on earth. But he and his people also knew that the magnificent honey they produced was worth a million stings. Above, he heard excited squawks and screams from a troop of chimpanzees. Only once had he seen chimps harvest honey, and many of the elders still do not believe him. As he looked he saw a dozen chimps hanging at precarious angles from topmost branches of a sapele tree, many carrying large sticks and beating the hives. Swarms of bees went on counterattack. From the heart of the aerial battlefield, one large hive was loosed and plunged to the forest floor. Kaluki rushed at it, sweeping off some very dazed bees and rushed off to enjoy such a magnificent dessert. As he retreated, he mouthed a grateful thanks to the chimps.

So with renewed energy, he walked on. Here in his forest he had always felt so safe, until yesterday when the impossible happened. In many parts of Africa, Kaluki's people called themselves Batwa. *Twa* means "just" or "only" in the sense of "it's only me" or "it's just the wind blowing." The harmless innocent one. Perhaps the perfect weakness of Dr. Obed's prayer in Camp Hopeful. Can God's strength be shown or even perfected in such weakness?

Kaluki stopped near a small new helicopter pad clearing prepared by these new strange ones. He stood beside a little mound of twigs and leaves under which his wife was buried. Asenath had always been very beautiful, more golden brown than coffee brown, with a heart of pure honey. She had given him two strong sons and two daughters, golden like their mother. He shuddered as he looked down.

The MaButi people had of course spoken of the wicked Interahamwe from Rwanda, who had murdered more people than there were stars in the black African sky. But they had never dared enter Ituri Forest...until yesterday. Then he had seen some of them with a strange new tribe. These people were much bigger and better fed. They had beaked noses and were multicolored: white and coffee and black people speaking many new languages. The BaButi feared them and had told him to watch out when they were around. Yesterday, he had been smoking a mix of tobacco and marijuana in his pipe made of bamboo stem with a strange unique pouch attachment made of ebony wood. His friend Tomas had also witnessed the kidnapping of his wife. Much later they found her deep in the forest. She was still tied by vines to a goat, which had frantically hauled her all over the forest floor. As he pondered on her final words to him, he was again overcome with guilt that he had not been there to help and a fierce anger that he had never known before.

"Many strange animals devoured me my love, many ..."

As Kaluki crouched, the whirring wings of the white man's bird became louder and louder.

What is going on? he thought. *Here they are again.* He watched as men and two women emerged. The bird immediately took off again. Then he recognized him. Him.

A little fearful Kaluki approached the group and gave the hornbill's cry. After a few moments, he heard the echo. Now with confidence, he approached them.

"Ibrahim?"

Ibrahim went forward, and in the staccato click language of the pygmies, he greeted his friend.

"Ibrahim's only real contact in this wilderness. This is Kaluki, who has helped us in the past." Dorcas introduced the group. "He says his wife was murdered by the strange tribe who have arrived here. He saw some arrive by chopper, and yes, a white girl and young black girl were with them."

Winslow gasped. "This is one of their safe havens. Oh God, help us!"

Kaluki was now speaking at speed. *Click, click, click.*

"What's he say now?"

Ibrahim smiled. "He says they are likely watching the landing place of the white man's bird. Even now. He says he will take us to his safe place."

"Does he have any idea where they took Eleanor and Kiabo?" Dorcas asked.

"Yes, he does. You see he becomes almost invisible in his forest. His two sons have learned all his forest craft, and they followed them and can show us, but first, we need to go the safe place, his own safe place."

"How does Ibrahim know this forest and Kaluki?" Willow asked.

Dorcas shook her head. "Long, long story. We seem to be fighting terror all around us in Uganda. Ibrahim was sent in when the Rwandan genocidaires were hiding outside the forest and planning cross-border raiding. He then went back and brought out Kiabo. He met with Kaluki and learned some of his click language. He's brilliant. A genius in fact. Much more useful and powerful than any AR 15 or AK 47. Funny, he has hardly uttered a word since escaping Somalia and now he's in full-flow bushman language!"

The group stood and listened to the sounds of the forest around them, then Dorcas Isiku continued speaking

"Far from the madding crowd, eh? Far too from the Brits' MI6, America's CIA, Russia's SVR, and even far from the best of the bunch the fearful and most ruthless intelligence agency formerly of King Saul Boulevard Tel Aviv. But today not even the Israeli prime minster seems to know its location. This is the perfect safe haven. And thanks to the miracle of Ibrahim's baby GPS, here we are. The GPS has also tracked the helicopter that took off from here to a remote part of Central African Republic, where there is likely another safe haven."

"Have our SEALs been given the coordinates?" Winslow asked. He wondered how Jeannie was taking all this and sent a prayer of support to D. C.

Col. Ben Tumusiime nodded. "Their Tilt Rotor was sent up to Juba from Entebbe, and they will now fly directly here when it arrives for them."

Kaluki indicated that all should follow him and fast. The next hours were especially hard on Willow and Winslow, twisting and turning into the forest and over small, almost invisible, streams.

What had the governor of the Bank of Uganda told him? Winslow thought. Centum. A hundred forests and a hundred streams. The largest of these, the Ituri River, fed into the great Congo River itself. Some of their footfalls startled tea-green butterflies feeding on vegetation on the forest floor. They rose in their hundreds in front of their faces. Kaluki blinked, brushed them aside, but did not break his stride. In contrast to Kaluki's silent stride, the others seemed to him more like a herd of frantic buffaloes. The noise likely attracted the real thing. Without warning, a forest buffalo crashed through a thicket of shrubs and headed toward them. Winslow grabbed Willow and pushed her down into a small stream that they were crossing. Kaluki dipped an arrow in poison from the little pouch, took aim, and fired. The arrow pierced the buffalo's right eye and stuck there. Without breaking stride, the buffalo swerved in confusion away from the group into a large protruding rock.

Kaluki now indicated that they must now proceed much faster.

"Thought he killed it?" Winslow murmured.

"An excellent shot but it takes hours for the poison to take effect," Ibrahim explained to the chairman of the Federal Reserve (acting, acting).

As they picked up pace, Willow tripped on a rotting branch lying on their path. She crashed into the undergrowth as thousands of butterflies rose in protest.

"I can't go any further," Willow told Winslow. "You know we go to the gym and all that, but this makes me realize how soft and really unfit most of us in the Western world are. Leave me here."

As she sat down, an animal with zebra-striped rear legs and strange short neck appeared and stared in wonderment at these new creatures.

"What's that?"

Dorcas pulled Willow to her feet. "Called an okapi giraffe. Unique to this forest. No need for a long neck like the Savannah giraffe since all her food is low lying."

"Leave me," Willow said again.

"That I would never do," he told her. He looked into her weary eyes. "Never ever," he told her.

"Where's Kaluki?" Dorcas asked.

The group looked around, but there was no sign of their guide.

"Oh God, now we're lost, really lost." In her exhaustion, Willow was becoming hysterical.

Winslow pulled her to him. "Shh, shh. Remember your great character slave girl, Florence. Samuel Baker said, 'She's not a screamer.'" His arms held her. Through their sweat-soaked clothes, her braless breasts tingled erect into his chest. They peered into each other's eyes. Neither blinked. A deep silence filled Ituri Forest. The buffalo, now far from them, dozed, awaiting his final breath. Kaluki's people would feast on him soon. Very little light now penetrated the gigantic forest canopy. Suddenly Willow broke from his embrace, startled as a bird that flutters from any sound of danger as from above, without warning, came the first ominous rumble of thunder heralding the arrival of the lifeline of the forest—rain. The office floor was then illuminated by gleaming rods of light. The next clap of thunder made them all jump. It appeared to be right on top of them. Then they were washed in what can only be described as a waterfall of rain—hard, relentless.

"Where's Kaluki?" Willow kept asking.

Ibrahim spoke softly. "He has gone to his high thinking place. It is his way."

*****

Kaluki sat alone on a large outcrop of rock above the forest line and looked skyward. He knew that he desperately needed help, wisdom, insight; and he knew that this only came from such aloneness and reflection. Very few people have seen what he was looking at, but scientists have recently documented the phenomenon. High above the fury of this violent thunderstorm, ghost riders flickered and danced like vanishing hallucinations. Kaluki asked the sprites, the elves, the fauns, the fairies in the sparkling sky what he should do next. The answer was dramatic. He saw something he himself had never seen before. Above the storm, a single streak of lightning shot straight up, not down but up, into the African dark sky. The battle described by Robert Kirk in his little treatise *The Secret Commonwealth of Elves, Fauns and Fairies* to be acted out, and victory achieved in the air between the good and evil spirits had begun. Would subsequent victory be achieved?

"Thank you," Kaluki said simply. "Thank you."

He then consulted with a small group of his people snuggled safe in their beehive-shaped homes.

The group had now no idea which direction to go.

*****

Ibrahim gave the hornbill call. No reply.

"Again, Ibrahim," Dorcas said urgently.

Ibrahim put his finger to his mouth indicating that deep forest silence was essential. Voices were coming closer.

Willow was now muttering to herself hysterically, "*Kanya ma kan*. Once upon a time. God help us all."

Chapter

16

The voices grew closer. Willow snuggled deeper into Winslow's embrace. The forest dripped water. Three men emerged from the undergrowth.

"Thank God it's Kaluki," Ibrahim said as he greeted Kaluki and his two sons.

The staccato of their conversation melded into the sounds of the storm-buffeted equatorial rain forest. *Click, click, click.* The three pygmies and Kaluki chatted like long-lost friends.

"Weird. The silent one now in full Churchillian flow," Dorcas said.

Kaluki indicated that they should follow him. They climbed up a steep slope. Winslow turned and saw below them a huge inland lake of water perfectly round with steep sides. Kaluki whispered with reverence, and Ibrahim translated.

"At the beginning of time heaven dropped her rock and then rains filled it up."

"Maybe a meteor," Dorcas said.

"This water has no bottom."

"Deep," said Dorcas.

"No," Ibrahim corrected her translation. "No. No bottom. Bottomless."

Still they climbed and then followed Kaluki through dense rubber vines into a large cave. There they all sat exhausted while

Kaluki lit a fire and began preparing forest mushrooms, grubs, and smoked antelope stew.

"Great restaurant!" Willow groaned at Winslow.

In her hysteria, Winslow felt an urgent need to protect her. He thought of his mother. "You've all I've got," he remembered her words to him. Though not convinced himself, he silently told her not to worry, he was coming back with her great-granddaughter.

Col. Ben Tumusiime and Dorcas shared some army rations, bottles of water, and they all ate a little.

Then Ibrahim translated all that Kaluki was saying.

"He says the girls are on an island in the middle of the lake."

"Oh, thank God," Winslow shouted. "Alive?"

"Yes, alive. He says there are preparations for execution..." Ibrahim could not continue.

Then it dawned on Dorcas what was happening. "At some point before the drone strike in Somalia, Ibrahim was to be beheaded. They screamed these words at him, 'Kanya ma kan.' And then the drone strike saved him." Now that he was talking, she desperately wanted to question him much more. But there was no time.

Ibrahim said simply, "Kaluki has a plan."

As he spoke lightning sparked through the forest canopy followed by deep rumbling of thunder and more torrential rain.

"Kaluki said, 'Good. Rain. This will help us.'"

Col. Tumusiime insisted that Willow and Winslow stay in the cave while he, Col. Sam Mulindwa, Maj. A. B. Mbonye, Maj. Dorcas Isiku, and Maj. Ibrahim Nabukenya go with Kaluki to implement the plan.

"Guess we're not needed," Willow murmured.

"Scared?"

"Petrified."

They both stared through the vines at the black African night.

"Every leaf seems weeping. Down the boles and branches, creepers and vegetable cords, the moisture trickles and falls on us."

"What the hell are you talking about?" Willow giggled.

"Just a quote from Henry Morton Stanley's *Through the Dark Continent.*"

Smoke from the fire drifted above them. Some of the vines covering the entrance to the cave now entwined parts of the ceiling. Some drops of thick sticky white milky secretion sap fell on Winslow's arm and stuck to his skin. He turned up his nose and rubbed it off.

"Caoutchoue," Willow said.

"Caoutchoue, caoutchoue, what a lovely word," Winslow replied.

"No, it's not," said Willow. "A South American Indian word. The Belgians then introduced it into their French language. It means the wild rubber vine. Produces fabulous latex. The Indian word literally means 'wood that weeps.' The weeping was not just for the vine but for the whole of Congo. The Belgians enslaved people to gather the wild rubber. If the day's quota was not met, then the Force Publique chopped of their hands."

Winslow pulled some more from his skin. "Horrible," he muttered.

"Since we're not exactly going anywhere fast without Kaluki, tell me that innermost secret of yours."

Willow looked at the concentric circles on the cave wall.

"After Robert, Bobby's, death I focused my work on children. But more than that, I did it for my mother. Her mother, who would have been my grandmother, died when my mother was only eight. Her father remarried and had five more kids. My mother became their nurse and really lost her own childhood. She told me all this on her death bed. She was an orphan who lost a childhood, so I do this work now in her memory. And yours?"

Winslow froze. Sharing was far from his daily routine. Hesitantly at first, then faster he spoke.

"After my dream, I found my dad near Pequot Island. His face. His face, Willow, was so tortured. I can't imagine what he had gone through. I...despite it all, I still love him, you know."

Willow held him close. Steam rose from their shirts as the fire warmed them. Drops of water fell into the flames and sizzled.

"Shh, shh. Thank you for sharing. Thank you."

Suddenly Winslow asked a question that had just popped into his mind.

"Vanity of vanities. Know what it means?" he asked. "Governor of the Bank of England used the expression when talking of the demise of my predecessor."

Willow grinned. "Thought you said your grandpa was a preacher? It's from the book of Ecclesiastes, the preacher. Chapter 1:1, I think. My favorite book in the Bible, by the way. He doesn't mention God much but gets pretty close to figuring out life's conundrums. Vanity is a bubble that bursts. He says we often chase after wind and get nowhere."

"That's true enough," Winslow agreed. "I don't care about anything now except Eleanor and getting her home to my mother."

"Even the chairmanship of the Fed?" Willow teased.

"Even the chairmanship of the Fed," Winslow replied slowly and seriously.

"Wonder why Kaluki helps us?"

"Well, he loves Ibrahim, and he probably would like to get some revenge for the torture and murder of his wife."

"Revenge, just like Abu."

A rustle of vines at the cave entrance.

"Who's there?" Willow shook with fear and hysteria.

Dorcas crawled into the cave.

"Phew! The Kampala marathon will be a picnic compared to this Ituri Forest gym."

She sat by the little fire and munched into a forest mango from a pile Kaluki had left. Deep orange juice ran down her cheeks. Then she became wistful.

"Dr. Obed will have finished the camp clearing by now and will be back to his day job at Christ the Healer Hospital."

"You're missing him a lot," Willow said.

"My life is too crazy. But on the other hand, we can't all just sit and count numbers like Mr. Winslow!"

Winslow scowled and then smiled. "I haven't given the Dow or any number a thought since I arrived in Africa," he said.

"Well, listen, this is not a social call. We need your help. We all need your help right away?"

Willow and Winslow looked at each other, surprise showing on their faces.

"Us?"

Dorcas then explained all that Kaluki had achieved so far.

"Kaluki threw his stones, then read them. Like some others of his people, Kaluki has 'the knowing.' It is hard to explain, but it is a knowledge which is beyond our simple senses of touching, seeing, hearing, smelling, and tasting. He saw back into this cave and said he was at peace because although *mzee* had lost his old wife, he has now found his new wife."

"Mzee?" Willow asked.

Dorcas smiled. "The old respected one. Guess that's you, Winslow!"

Willow glanced at Winslow, then suppressed another hysterical giggle.

"Kaluki has explained the plan to Col. Tumusiime. On the little island, he saw many beehive houses, you know, the pygmy houses of his people, which they make in a day, stay for a while, then move on. A bit like the huge tree nests of the mountain gorillas."

"Airbnb," Willow muttered. Her hysteria was now at its height. "Airbnb, Airbnb."

Dorcas ignored her. "They are empty now, but since his people cannot swim, he wondered how they got there to build and sleep. He asked some of them and has found one small straight shallow wetlands ridge about three feet deep at the north end of the island. He and the soldiers will go through it. The ISIS people have one large canoe moored at a small pier this south end of the island, but it is guarded. He needs someone to swim underwater undetected to that canoe and bring it round to the eastern side to pick everyone up."

"That's it?" asked Willow. "That's it!"

"Well, it's step one. Kaluki can't swim. I can't swim. The Ugandan soldiers say it's not their strongest suit."

Willow walked over to the cave entrance and stared down to the lake. "Hell of a distance from here to the pier. About fifty meters. Wonder how long it would take to swim it and underwater?"

Winslow shrugged his shoulders. "Two minutes, the lung's limit, or it won't work." *Thank you, Grandpa,* he thought.

Willow looked at him. "You. Can you do that?"

Winslow thought of his most recent dream of his grandfather on the West Sands of St. Andrews. "Breath, laddie, breath. Our most valuable gift."

"Yes, I could try," he replied.

"No way!" Willow objected. "No, no. Too dangerous."

"I need Eleanor's forgiveness, and I can't receive that without bringing her out of here."

Without another word Winslow and Dorcas made their way down through the deep vegetation clinging to the steep sides of the crater lake. Willow watched them go and then returned to the cave.

*****

Eight ISIS/al-Qaeda fighters, veterans from Iraq, Iran, England, Egypt, and Syria sat in a huge tent that was struggling to keep out rainwater from the storm. Their other two comrades were drenched and guarding their canoe with outboard motor. Carefully selected, they were committed to the final battle against the infidel and specifically the Great Satan and his junior devils. Several Interahamwe thugs for hire were preparing a fire and cooking. Nine other sites with ten fighters had been carefully selected throughout the world; and the centum, the hundred, were now ready, ready to give themselves in the final battle.

Eleanor huddled in a corner of the tent with Kiabo slumped on top of her.

Her fainting is such a blessing, Eleanor thought. "Sleep, dear friend, just sleep," she murmured.

The radical offshoot of the caliphate talked in Arabic, English, Aramaic; but to Eleanor's ears, it was all babel. Every so often they would point and jeer at the girls. Eleanor recalled Kiabo's story of gang rape, and she shuddered and held Kiabo tighter than ever. Then the tent flap moved. Eleanor froze. A hand pulled it open. Eleanor stared into the eyes of the world's number one terror suspect—Abu.

He stumbled toward her.

"It is written," he said simply. "It is written. 'A life for a life.' So you are the little American girl. My own daughter Amina, she died in your evil drone strike. Now you will die. It is written, 'a life for a life.'"

Eleanor held Kiabo even tighter as she stuttered to herself, "We need you now, Ibrahim. Please help as you helped dear Kiabo."

"Ibrahim? Is he still alive?" This news had a chilling effect on Abu. He shook Eleanor's shoulders. "Is he? He knows too much."

"Yes, no, I mean, he is very sick after the torture," Eleanor muttered.

Abu suddenly seemed very deflated. Of course, he had said too much to Ibrahim, but he had been on the point of death. Now Ibrahim alive was bad news. He alone held his deepest secret. Then seconds later, suddenly revived, he rushed from the tent, screaming, "Prepare for the execution, now! I will lead it!"

Chapter

17

Dorcas and Winslow made their way carefully down through the steep undergrowth to the water's edge. They were now hidden behind a bush overhanging the warm waters of the crater lake.

"What is it the Germans say? 'Go with God but go!'" Dorcas muttered.

Then thanking his grandfather, Winslow took a deep breath, taking in all the beautiful life-giving oxygen his lungs could hold and slid under the still waters. Dorcas moved swiftly up the slopes and stood outside the cave. She then gave her version of the call of the African gray hornbill. *Pi-pipi*...accelerating ascending, then descending into a rather sad *pipipipi-pieu-pieu*. It moved over the waters. Not as perfect as Kaluki's, but...silence. Surely Kaluki's sharp ears had heard? Or was old age catching up with him? Dorcas decided not to repeat the call.

Then it came back. Clear and hopeful. *Pipipipipipipi-pieu-pieu*. The sign.

The torrential rain had now slackened to a steady mist, perfect for jungle orchids but miserable for *homo sapiens*. Dorcas joined Willow in the cavern. She added some more wood to the fire and blew to encourage the flames to leap. The two women huddled close for comfort, staring into the dancing flames.

"Thank God I stopped teaching," Dorcas murmured into the dancing flames.

Willow shrugged. She stared at the concentric circles on the cave wall. They turned in front of her. Entranced. In a trance. Hysteria never far from the surface.

"No point at all," continued Dorcas, "without security, decent governance, security and decent governance. Don't we all deserve that? Doesn't lovely Kiabo deserve that?"

Willow's head now revolved with the clockwise spinning circles on the cave wall.

"Mmm," she murmured.

Dorcas now started shouting. "It's too hard, Willow. Too complicated. Imagine, with peace Obed and I could live together, healing and teaching. But oh no, instead we have these idiot wars!"

*****

Back in Washington, D. C., Jeannie Backhouse was at her desk, or rather pacing around it. If her PA had thought she had been jumpy some days ago, she would have called it calm compared to this morning. As she strode up and down, the secretary of state muttered to Thomas Jefferson's grandfather clock outside the door of her office and to her own grandfather's grandfather clock in the office corner.

"A trillion dollars we've spent since 9/11. A thousand billion frickin' dollars. Spook agencies, thousands of new skyscrapers to house them, private contractors all chasing the bottomless dollar harvest, buckets full of information overload that no one can handle or synthesize, and what do we get?"

Both clocks struck the hour and played the Westminster chimes in perfect unison.

"Exactly. Zilch! Nada! We get the chairman of the Federal Reserve lost in frickin' Congo among al-Qaeda with supporting cast of local rebel groups!"

God help me she's talking to herself now. Wonder if the new Reserve Starbucks on Connecticut Avenue needs a trainee barista?

The secretary of state's PA quaked in her cube.

"Tami!"

167

"Ma'am."

"Tami! Ambassador Jimmy now!"

"Ma'am."

"Jimmy. Where is the Tilt Rotor Osprey?"

Ambassador Jimmy Marsh had canceled all golf games and even a special cocktail party for his wife's International Women's Association. His wife had cut down his daily alcohol intake and now woke him early each day to throw him out with his driver to the American Embassy. Crises have a way of sharpening the edge of all of our faculties. Ambassador Jimmy Marsh stood to attention to take the call.

"Preparation for takeoff from Juba South Sudan, ma'am, almost complete. ETA Ituri Forest in twenty minutes. Defence Attaché Wallace Willard is now with Delta Force. He went up with the Tilt."

"So including our defence attaché, five SEALs?"

"Yes, ma'am."

"I understand we have the GPS location of a second site in Central African Republic?"

"Yes, ma'am."

"Now ordinarily, and God knows life is never ordinary, ordinarily—what am I talking about? Who the hell ever says *ordinarily* anymore! Ordinarily, we could proceed to drone strike both sites. However, the chairman of the Federal Reserve is in an impenetrable Congo forest and his granddaughter is being held hostage at one of these sites."

The ambassador's hand shook as he poured some of his deep-secret office store of Jack Daniels into his empty coffee cup. *I don't believe this. What the hell happened to my final fun-filled peaceful posting?* "I will keep you appraised as things develop, ma'am."

"Moment by small moment, Jimmy. Second by small second. Day or night. Please cancel any thoughts of sleeping."

"Yes, ma'am."

The American ambassador to Uganda looked sadly at his now depleted Jack Daniels bottle.

*****

Winslow swam with slow deliberate breaststrokes submerged several feet below the lake surface. After each stroke, he moved his arms to his side as he glided forward. He could still hear his grandfather's words. "Glide, laddie, glide. No effort. Just enjoy the result of each breaststroke."

For US SEALs, the training for this part of their initiation is carefully supervised since it often results in sudden blackouts and in some cases even death. For Winslow in the depths of this Ituri Forest crater lake, there was no such safety net.

Each stroke was a request for forgiveness from his granddaughter. Each stroke was a grim determination to do what Sir Jeremy had advised, "See life in perspective and ask himself what really, really mattered." Each stroke formed a far-from-perfect pearl, a wild baroque pearl but more valuable than perfectly-formed farmed mother of pearl, a lovely wild pearl, beyond value, priceless. Sixty seconds passed. Winslow counted each stroke as Grandpa had instructed, to give an estimation of time and distance.

*****

Kaluki's discussion with some of his people who had spent time on the island had been extremely helpful. The Batwa knew each nook and cranny of their forest. For each of them, it was their livelihood, their security, their passion, their home.

"Look out for the lily trotters. Their nests are the start of the ridge pathway."

Kaluki led the Ugandan soldiers and Ibrahim down the northern slopes of the lake. Several brown-and-black birds with white necks each with black stripes were walking over large lily leaves. Their large feet enabled them to walk as if on the forest floor. Kaluki looked closer and saw a nest. He spoke to Ibrahim, who was gasping for breath as he had just rejoined the group.

"He says the mother is off in search of food and the father sits on the eggs."

"You mean the mother sits on the eggs," Col. Ben Tumusiime corrected him.

Maj. A. B. Mbonye laughed. "No, the father. You see, the female lily trotter is a liberated bird. My wife's favorite bird!"

Kaluki felt carefully in the water with his feet. A small cascading stream entered the lake, and the sediment was clearly forming the ridge. Concentric circles formed as the water dropped down. *The cave sign*, he thought excitedly. *And the straight walking place, like the light that streaks upward.* Kaluki expressed his gratitude at nature's signs by bowing his head toward the watery undergrowth. He gingerly moved on and indicated that all should follow. Step by slow deliberate step they made their way toward the island. Every so often Kaluki made them stop while he listened with his ears and his knowing. This north side of the island was totally quiet and uninhabited. Behind the little group there was a gentle splash as the father lily trotter took a break from his maternal duties and went in search of his own food. They all looked back. Each sound seemed magnified in the silent pond. When Maj. A. B. Mbonye looked forward again, he was shocked to see that Kaluki was no longer in front of him.

"What! Where? Kaluki's gone. Oh God, help us."

*****

Winslow estimated that maybe ninety seconds had passed. Bubbles slowly moved to the surface as his one breath was giving out and an insane desire to breathe again encompassed all other thoughts. His grandfather muttered to him.

"Breath is life, laddie. Breath at creation, breath giving recovery from viral infection, breath at the birthday of the Kirk at Pentecost, breath in your life and mine. Breath is everything."

He was now sure he could go no further. It was one thing as a young man to practice this, but hell, he was now Social Security age! He decided to slowly surface. As he rose, he saw his own father's face. Not the anguished face at Pequot Island. He was smiling. Smiling at him. A deep peace infused his whole being.

Forgiveness given and accepted. Perfect peace. Then his nose broke the surface. Deep beautiful life-giving air. He luxuriated in every breath, filling and refilling his depleted lungs. He looked ahead and saw very little at first. As his eyes adjusted to the forest darkness, he could see the cigarettes of the two guards as they chatted with backs to him, looking into the island in the direction of their makeshift and temporary camp. Then he saw the outline of a large canoe with outboard motor. He swam slowly toward it and nestled behind its frame. He waited as instructed by Ibrahim, or rather as instructed by Kaluki with Ibrahim's translation. And waited. And waited. He stood waist deep and began to shiver even though he was near the equator and the light rain was warmish. "Shock," he told himself. Then from behind the canoe, he heard the voices of the two al-Qaeda guards laughing as they turned and walked quickly toward their boat. Winslow huddled closer to the boat till he felt each protruding barnacle tickle his skin.

Chapter

18

Up in the cave, Willow's hysteria had abated. She now lay slumped on the cave floor. Beside her, Dorcas sat quietly, looking at the bushman paintings on the walls. Neither spoke for some time.

Then Willow spoke slowly and softly. "I had no idea what your boys were going through in Somalia. Poor Ibrahim. I'm sorry. Thank God for the drone strike."

Dorcas poked the fire to encourage the flames and added a few more broken branches to it. "I need to speak to the boss."

"Col. Ben Tumusiime?"

"Yes, the boss."

"New information?"

"Perhaps. Ibrahim has been closed as a clam in deep wet sand since his arrival in the Ugandan Army Camp outside Mogadishu. But now he's opening up. Seems that he was able to dig up a little pouch containing what he had hidden before his capture."

"The GPS?"

"Yes, but there is something else, and he just won't say."

"'And aye keep somethin' to yourself,'" Willow murmured.

"Late at night, after everyone else had gone to sleep, Kiabo brought him over to me and encouraged him to open up a bit. He told me he can't swim. Then he spoke of his water boarding. They mocked him and said they learned it in Abu Ghraib. Then they poured petrol on his arms and legs and lit a match. Next day was to be his beheading. And all the time they yelled, 'Centum!' and told him the password, 'Kanya ma kan.' As he spoke to me, his whole body shook, and he wept waterfalls of tears. Never seen a man break just like that. But there's something else, Willow. I know there is, but I don't know what."

Willow shivered. A few bats, now disturbed by the storm cacophony outside, swirled around the cave walls. She held her hair, petrified at the thought of one of them choosing such a perch.

"I wonder if Obed has closed camp by now and will be back at his Christ the Healer Hospital?"

"He's lovely. You two are so different but made for each other, you know."

"Opposites attract, eh?"

"Mmm. Like bees to pollen."

"What do you mean?"

"Pollen is negatively charged and, therefore, are attracted to any positive charge. Bees are positively charged and are attracted to flowers with the strongest negative charges."

"Last night Obed did, in his stuttering way, broach the topic of marriage."

"Oh?"

"I told him, 'No more words please,' said yes, and kissed him."

"Oh, congratulations. That's great news."

"Thank you. I was wondering if, well, if we ever get the hell out of here, if you would be my maid of honor?"

"Would be an honor."

The fire illuminated the room. Willow watched the dancing light and thought of all that had happened to her in such a short period of time since that first airport kiss.

"Winslow kissed me, you know?" She then shared the airport story that led to their journey together to Africa.

"Surely more than a coincidence all that, isn't it? I mean, it's fate."

"And as you say, opposites have strong magnetic attraction."

As Willow stared out of the cave door into the dark night, she saw clearly the bright morning star Venus rising in the east heralding a new day. A few moments later she thought she saw a hint of morning. Nothing special or spectacular, just a hint of the sky being a little less dark. She thought back to some of her mother's musings. Nyx, the great goddess of the night and mother of primordial darkness, was at the cave door ready to welcome her daughter Hemera, goddess of day. The philosopher David Hume said that there was no guarantee that morning would come just because it had so frequently in the past. Therefore, we should all be aware of the uncertainty and general transient nature of our lives. Her mother had always loved quoting that. Uncertainty is our middle name, isn't it? Willow thought of her own future and, of course, the extraordinary meeting with Winslow. The moneyman had more depth than she had at first given him credit for. And he was promising to write a tome on inequality after all. But was he husband material? She smiled to herself at this turn of phrase, part of the wine-drenched conversation of girlfriends. Could she trust him? She looked at Dorcas and decided to ask her opinion.

"Is he husband material?"

Dorcas's screams of laughter filled the cave. Bats galore swooped in consternation at such a question.

"Husband material! You make him sound like a spark plug in an outboard motor! If you do end up a couple, don't try to adjust the timing of the engine. Men are men. They are incorrigible, unchangeable, hey but also gorgeous."

The two women laughed. Dorcas stared at the *okapi* running and the *BaTwa* spears chasing them on the wall. The spinning concentric circles made her dizzy, and she looked down and poked the embers. A few sparks flew upwards into the dark cave ceiling.

Despite David Hume's misgivings, the sky was imperceptibly lightening.

*****

Fast. Decisive. It was Col. Ben Tumusiime who reacted first.

"Stepped off the ridge."

He pushed past Maj. A. B. Mbonye and fished in the gurgling water. Then he pulled Kaluki straight out like a cork from a wine bottle. *Plop.* He almost laughed out loud at so bedraggled and miserable a creature. Kaluki shook water from his body like a golden Labrador after a seaside plunge. He checked his bow and precious satchel, soaked but intact. Then regaining his dignity, he led the little group to the final yards of the island. They moved cautiously forward.

After about fifty yards, Kaluki indicated that they should stop and wait. He climbed a nearby tree with an alacrity that belied his years. In the branches, he closed his eyes and listened. Two sounds, at least two sounds, for his trained ears. First, there was a quite lyrical *krrrou* varying at regular intervals of six seconds. He opened his eyes and saw that an African scops owl was staring unblinking at him. *Another important source of wisdom.* Athena, goddess of wisdom and of war, made sure that the owl was the world's first protected species. All combatants knew that this presence on the eve of battle ensured final victory. As she sat patiently waiting for the telltale scurry of mice, snakes, or any potential food on the forest floor, Kaluki smiled at her. The second sound was further away but so familiar. Kaluki knew it immediately. He smacked his lips at the sound of buzzing. The African bees were settling into their large hives high in the branches of an ebony tree some distance beyond the owl. Beneath them he could see the open flaps of the tarpaulin and the Islamist fighters inside. One of them walked out with a cigarette in his mouth. In all his years Kaluki had never killed another person. All the poison he had gathered had been to harvest fast food for himself and his family. His little pouch was his McDonald's Grubhub order. But in these last few days, things had changed. His wife, Asenath, was dead. He had seen the heat-mangled scars on the legs and arms of his friend Ibrahim and now two young people's lives were in danger. Kaluki's world had changed, and the clarity of what must happen next flashed into his consciousness.

*****

Kiabo was now awake in the tent as Eleanor told her about the visitation.

"They are going to kill us," Eleanor said. "And don't tell me you still believe in forgiveness."

Kiabo shrugged. "Well, at least forgive your poor grandpa who came looking for you," she suggested.

"I'll think about it. Kiabo?"

"Mmm."

"Kiabo. Tell me your secret."

"What do you mean?"

"Well, I mean life hasn't exactly been a bed of roses for you, but you always seem so calm, almost joyful at times."

Despite their predicament, Kiabo smiled. "Dunno. In my worst moments, I see light, glory, the very face of God. And he's always smiling, encouraging me onwards."

"Well, tell him to come in here now," Eleanor moaned.

The tent flap opened, and Abu beckoned for the girls to follow him. He turned to lead them out. As Kiabo watched his receding head, fury welled up in her—fury at life's unfairness, fury at her HIV infection, fury at the death of her brother and new boyfriend in the Entebbe bombing. Fury. A rarified scorched earth primal fury. She picked up a rock from the cave floor; and stumbling toward Abu with a scream, she hurled the rock, David-to-Goliath like, at Abu as he turned back in astonishment. It struck him above his nose, and he fell forward onto the floor of the cave, cursing and moaning.

"Hit him again, Kiabo," Eleanor screamed.

Kiabo turned, looking for another missile.

Too late. Abu, blood streaming over his eyes, grabbed her leg and held her.

*****

Kaluki came down and gave final instructions to Col. Ben and his colleagues. He also had a special mission for Ibrahim. Returning up the sapele tree, he prepared wet, but still potent, poison on one of his arrow tips, a quantity larger than the buffalo amount, and took aim at the nearest fighter and fired. Straight. Accurate. Deadly.

Dropping his cigarette, the Egyptian screamed, dropped to the ground, and lay there, desperately clutching the arrow, which penetrated the side of his eye socket. Immediately after this, Kaluki restrung his bow with a single arrow and fired it into the larger of the two hives. This was followed by a second toward the other hive. The next subsequent movement was from the African scops owl who took off, glided silently through the resultant chaos, snapping a few bees en route as an hors d'oeuvre and headed off to a more peaceful hunting perch. Chaos ensued. The scream of pain was followed by voices of consternation. There was a stampede out of the tent. The angry bees went on their most vicious attack. Col. Ben then lugged two grenades into the melee.

This was the sign for Winslow, who began to breathe more freely as the guards left their post and rushed back to camp. *What the hell kept you all!*

Winslow clambered into the canoe, released the line, and pulled on the outboard starter handle. A little chug but no energy. *Shit.* He tried again. A little splutter. *Plugs, probably soaked from all the deluge.* He waited a few precious minutes and tried again. This time it caught, and the engine roared into life. *Thank you, God.* Winslow's prayer life was expanding exponentially. He then made his way round the island to the eastern rendezvous.

Major A. B. Mbonye made a surprise attack on the two guards coming from the shore, and Col. Ben Tumusiime and Col. Sam Mulindwa then began a major gun battle with the jihadists. For Ibrahim, who was used to his own anonymity, it was not so difficult to follow through on Kaluki's instructions and crawl under the back of the marquee. As he looked up, he saw Abu leaping forward, holding Eleanor's leg and now lunging at her with a knife.

177

"Abu!" he growled.

Abu stared at him, now frozen in time, knife held high above Eleanor.

"Alive? How? Ibrahim?"

"Back from the grave. To haunt you forever."

Ibrahim's fury now eclipsed that of Kiabo. His primal scream rent the forest air. "For jajja, for dear Kiabo, for Uganda!" His torture-scorched arms lifted Abu into the air and hurled him out among the staccato hurly-burly of AK47s, AR15s, and apoplectic African bees.

"Follow me! Now!" he commanded.

They needed no further encouragement. Swiftly the three made their way to the shore, trying to ignore the sound of warfare.

Ibrahim stopped and ushered the girls forward to the launch. Winslow stood in the boat and yelled encouragement. As Eleanor sprinted past Ibrahim toward the safety of the canoe, she tripped on the protruding roots of a sapele tree sapling. With a scream, she plunged forward.

"Catch me, Grandpa, catch me!" she yelled.

This time he did. Winslow opened his arms wide and caught her into the canoe. They crashed together among some fish heads at the bottom of the launch.

"This time you caught me, Grandpa. You caught me!" Eleanor yelled.

Grandfather and granddaughter clung to each other. Kiabo leapt in and clung to Willow. Colonel Ben and his colleague arrived with Col. Sam Mulindwa carrying Maj. A. B. Mbonye. They crashed into the boat, and Colonel Ben took the helm from Winslow. Ibrahim and Kaluki silently joined them. As they sped over the tranquil lake fifteen years of separation were eclipsed between grandfather and granddaughter.

"You came back, Grandpa," Eleanor murmured.

"Pink teddy will be pleased," Kiabo said.

"And so will your great-grandmother, Eleanor. We need to get back to her."

"Jajja, I am coming now with Ibrahim. We have so much to tell you," Kiabo whispered to young dawn's rose-red fingers.

*****

The next hours passed in an adrenalin-soaked haze. From the cave entrance, Willow and Maj. Dorcas Isiku descended to join the others. Winslow was carrying Eleanor.

"You did it?" Willow rushed over and hugged ecstatically. "You did it! How?"

"Don't sound so surprised."

Col. Ben Tumusiime now carried Maj. A. B. Mbonye. Col. Sam Mulindwa carried Kiabo, who insisted on walking from time to time. Major Dorcas Isiku helped Willow over some of the rough spots. Ibrahim walked with Kaluki, who led them carefully but swiftly back to the chopper landing site.

"Tilt Rotor is here, thank God," Dorcas yelled.

The American SEALs were superb. Caring, efficient, professional. They took Maj. A. B. Mbonye first into the chopper, then the others boarded. Within a brief period, they took off into the lightening morning sky.

The Tilt Rotor pushed above the forest and cloud line. Kiabo's wish to fly was now granted a second time but in much more glorious circumstances. The Tilt Rotor 22, with two expert pilots and five US Navy SEALs, was both secure and comfortable. The SEALs were proficient and very attentive to the needs of all of their passengers. The senior medic SEAL was treating Maj. A. B. Mbonye. After some time, he looked up. His ashen face told all of the passengers what had happened. He gently closed the major's eyes. They were all quiet. Then one soprano voice rose above the thrum and drum of the chopper's engines.

> Twas Grace that taught my heart to fear
> And Grace my fears relieved
> How precious did that grace appear
> The hour I first believed.
> Through many dangers, toils and snares
> We have already come
> T'was grace that brought us safe thus far
> And grace will lead us home.
> And grace will lead us home.

Winslow looked at Dorcas, the teacher-cum-extraordinary-tyrant-catcher. What would his grandfather have made of all this?

Of course, he had loved John Newton's hymn and it had often been sung in Duddington Kirk. But this morning, after the fury of warfare, the release of two lovely young people who had been held captive, the words were fresh.

"Through many dangers, toils and snares…"

ETA Entebbe, fifty-five minutes," the pilot announced.

"No."

It was the soprano singer who now spoke clearly. Dorcas Isiku yelled above the engine noise.

"For security reasons, we must return to Camp Hopeful now. Ibrahim insists. Immediately."

This was followed by a heated discussion, but after some time the SEALs accepted this strange decision.

"Nuts. Just nuts," one of them was heard murmuring. "But then that just about sums up our lives. Proceed to Juba in South Sudan. Proceed to Ituri Forest in Congo. Proceed to Kids' Camp Hopeful! Nuts. Just nuts!"

Everyone looked out of the Tilt windows as they swooped, fish eagle-like, toward Lake Albert.

As the flight plan altered and they descended toward the secondary source of the Nile, there was an announcement from the flight deck.

"Ladies and gentlemen, from the starboard, that is right-hand windows, you will see the fabled Rwenzori Mountain Range, the ancients' Mountains of the Moon. Despite global warming, Mount Margarita still has some glacial snows on her lovely head. I heard that some crazy Brits once had a fun skiing club up there."

Willow pushed over to look, her nose already touching the window. "Oh my God! This is so rare. Nearly always in cloud cover."

Winslow pushed past her to the window. "Just like your movie, eh?"

*****

Back at Camp Hopeful, Dr. Obed had said good-bye to the children but had kept the camp staff.

"Thought you were going back to Christ the Healer Hospital." Dorcas rushed toward Dr. Obed Ochola.

He swept her into his arms. "Had a premonition that Camp Hopeful wasn't ready to be closed yet, so I kept on the catering staff. I was right. Here you are. The pouch, eh?"

Dorcas nodded.

Back at Camp Hopeful everyone had a chance to shower, change clothes and rest a little. Winslow was delighted to find the balance of his Banana Republic outfit. Somehow, adrenaline still pumping in all of them meant that sleep was impossible. Pots of Sipi Falls coffee were served. Stories were exchanged.

Ibrahim told them all how he had left his friend Kaluki.

"I was the last to board the Tilt chopper. Kaluki took me to his wife Asenath's little grave. Two African gray parrots were sitting on the grave. 'Asenath,' they called in unison. 'Asenath.' Kaluki thanked them, and with a wink at me, he disappeared deep into his homeland, the great Ituri Forest. There he will join his little family as they move even deeper to safety."

"She was the Egyptian wife of Joseph in the book of Genesis," Dorcas said.

"Who?" Winslow asked.

"Asenath. It means peril or misfortune, so it is kind of appropriate given what happened to her in the end."

"So how did Kaluki choose that name?"

"Therein lies an even greater mystery, numbers man," Dorcas said with a grin.

Willow shook her head and smiled. "Wonderful," she muttered, "just wonderful."

Dorcas now pushed Ibrahim on all that he knew. "That little pouch of yours, Ibrahim. Come on, what else was in it?"

Ibrahim, the silent one in all languages with the exception of bushman lingo, left the group, walked over to a little spot behind the refectory tent, and dug with his hands beside an acacia sapling. He walked back and handed the pouch to Dorcas.

She pulled out a small memory stick.

"When the American drone strike happened, this was dropped. I grabbed it, retrieved my pouch from where I had hidden it. It still had my Ugandan Army GPS in it. I then popped this into it."

Dorcas took the memory stick. Everyone looked on with anticipation. What deep secrets did it contain? She carefully put it into a laptop. User name? Centum. Password? By now she already knew the answer. "Once upon a time." *Kanya ma kan?* The screen opened, showing page after page of one hundred faces and names. The hundred offshoots of the caliphate. Centum. Nothing else.

"The jihadis who will carry out the final destruction, the nuclear devices strikes on selected targets," Dorcas said.

"I need to send this over to our secretary of state, ASAP," Winslow said.

*****

"Done. Copy. Send attachment." He smiled as he saw Jeannie's face on receiving this. "I promise to assure her that when you are really close to the suffering, you learn so much. This is a great help with all our facial recognition devices at our ports and airports."

Winslow and Willow then made their way to the ridge over the lake.

"This is how the movie ends, Win."

Win? No one calls him Win except his mother.

Taking the manuscript from her, Winslow read.

*****

EXT. LAKE ALBERT SHINING IN THE SUN. 36 KILOMETERS ACROSS TO CONGO MOUNTAINS WITH WATERFALLS – CONTINUOUS
SAMUEL BAKER
A see-a huge inland African sea of quicksilver.
FLORENZ

Our prize, our own prize, dear Sam, bursts upon us!
Silence. Fish eagle hovers over the lake. A pack of baboons
come up the steep cliffs. They silently stare. Florence and Sam
kneel down.

SAMUEL BAKER
Lord, we thank Thee for having guided and supported
us through all dangers to this wonderful end.

Acholi song, again very softly. Lake so deep as morning star's
luck.

FLORENZ
(mischievously)
Ties ribbon round a branch
FLORENZ (CONT'D)
This lake is for Hungary. It will be called after my father general.

SAMUEL BAKER
(shakes his head in the negative and smiles)
As an imperishable memorial of the one loved and mourned
by our gracious queen Victoria, I name this lake Albert Nyanza.
The Victoria and Albert lakes are the twin sources of the Nile.

FLORENZ
So it shall be a tribute to faithful love.

Sam and Florence do not speak but stare into each other's eyes
while our theme tune again is heard.

CUT TO:

EXT. STEEP ESCARPMENT DOWN TO LAKE ALBERT

Florence starts to scramble down the steep escarpment. Sam
runs behind.

FLORENZ
For Hungary!
SAMUEL BAKER
For England! For Scotland!

Wonderful chaos as they scramble down. Colobus black-and-
white monkeys scream in trees above them. Baboons grunt and run
around. Saat, Richard, and others in the party come behind them,
laughing and shouting. The monkey, Wallady, clings to Saat, afraid

of the baboons. Monitor lizards slide away from their descent. Saat fires his rifle into the air. Arnout beats furiously on his drum. They reach the ground and a small sandy beach on lakeshore. Sam and Florence run into water together and dive deep. Come up laughing. Florence and Sam are both topless.

> FLORENZ
> Water, dear sweet water.

> SAMUEL BAKER
> Drink deeply my dear from the very heart of
> Africa, from the sources of the Nile.

Sam is looking to shore, and Florence looks behind her to south west.

> FLORENZ
> Sam, look, Montes Lunae, the Mountains of
> the Moon. And there is snow on top!

Clouds have cleared; and Mount Margarita, top of Rwenzori Mountains, is clear at 16,500 feet. A large snow-capped glacier is on top.

> SAMUEL BAKER
> (laughs)
> Still hallucinating, my dear. Is this Shakespeare's
> hot ice and wondrous strange
> snow you are seeing!

Sam turns around to southwest but clouds cover the peaks again.

> FLORENZ
> (disappointed)
> I saw snow, Sam, I swear.

> SAMUEL BAKER
> All right, let's have a snowball fight!

They begin throwing water at each other, and Florence screams. Sam laughs.

DISSOLVE TO:

TO:

EXT. LAKE ALBERT AGAIN. – DAY

Florence and Sam still naked from waist up, cavorting in the lake. In water, rainbow colors fade again to another fast-forward scene.

INT. BUCKINGHAM PALACE, LONDON. – AFTERNOON

Samuel is alone since Queen Victoria has not invited Florence. He kneels before his monarch, and she touches each of his shoulders with a large ceremonial sword.

QUEEN VICTORIA
Arise, Sir Samuel.

EXT. BACK TO LAKE ALBERT AGAIN. – DAY

†Sam picks Florence up in his arms and kisses her. Behind them clouds clear and we see Margarita peak again (16,500 feet) with snow on the glacier on top. This is the highest peak in the Rwenzori range of mountains to south of Lake Albert between Uganda and Congo. The fabled Montes Lunae, the Mountains of the Moon. This is freeze frame as credits appear. Same theme song is played quietly.

THE END

*****

"Beautiful, Willow. I'm impressed."

"Thank you. So a movie maybe?"

"Dunno. Talk to the adopted daughter of the movie mogul."

As if on cue, Eleanor strolled over with Kiabo in tow. Inseparable. Some white pearl-like pebbles spelled out BFF in the dust.

"Best friends forever," Eleanor assured Kiabo. "Soon after studies, you will be Nurse Kiabo." She turned to Winslow. "We came to say good-bye to the lake, our lake, properly this time." Eleanor took Winslow's hand and pulled him toward the lake. Then with her other hand, she grabbed Willow. "Come on, Jajja, hurry up!"

Jajja?

As marriage proposals, go this was surely the strangest.

"Jajja. Grandma?"

Willow looked at Winslow. Winslow looked at Willow. Like the African scops owl, neither blinked.

Winslow put his arms around Willow. "Maybe it's just post-traumatic stress disorder, maybe it's my excess adrenaline speaking. But hey, Willow, I don't want us to say good-bye after all this. I mean, Eleanor needs a third grandmother."

Not the most romantic speech. But then numbers men are not known for their poetry.

Willow looked up, and their lips met. Noses touched first, just like the airport kiss, then a longer lingering kiss.

After the horrors of the past forest hours, they clung to each other. Understanding that perhaps a little privacy was in order, Eleanor took Kiabo's hand and walked to the lake.

"Dorcas has asked me to be her bridesmaid."

"Does Dr. Ochola know about this marriage?"

"Men! Of course, he does. Well, I think so."

"Maybe she could also be yours."

"Is that a proposal?"

Winslow looked over the shimmering lake. "Albert Nyanza. Your movie says it's a tribute to faithful love, Florence, I mean, Willow."

"To the very heart of Africa."

"Two hearts as one."

They gazed beyond the sparkling lake. Bright sunshine illuminated the cloud cover now over the Rwenzoris, the Mountains of the Moon, in the Pearl of Africa. Many more mysteries would be part of their lives, but here in Africa's heart there was an understanding that these new incipient pearls would be theirs to explore together—forever.

The End